SAMSON

SAMSON

MEMORIES
OF A FOUND HOUND

CARMEN AMBROSIO

SAMSON: Memories of a Found Hound
AMBROSart, Ltd.
Dublin, Ohio 43017

www.ambrosart.com

ISBN 978-0-692-87108-9

Printed in the United States of America.

No association with any real company, product, person or event
is intended or should be inferred.

The following essay originally appeared in *Life Continues: Facing the
Challenges of MS, Menopause and Midlife with Hope, Courage and Humor*
in slightly different form: "Sammy Da Sage".

Library of Congress Control Number: 2017905903

For Sir Lawrence James

Table of Contents

Preface

In the pages that follow, I recount memorable morsels of life with my human mom, whom I call Mistress Carmen, and her husband, Master Larry—my human dad, usually patient walk leader, and pooper scooper. The tale shifts to my adventures in an otherworldly realm where dog spirits thrive.

Some of these pieces appeared previously online on my dog blog. Most have been updated to include new hound hindsight. Mistress also couldn't resist adding a few notes and odes as well as a chapter about me from her first book, a memoir, entitled *Life Continues: Facing the Challenges of MS, Meno-*

pause and Midlife with Hope, Courage and Humor. (That sub-title is so long that I used to snooze and snack before anyone finished saying it.)

Mistress and I hope you enjoy our collaboration.

Woof!

-Samson Ambrosio

SAMSON: MEMORIES OF A FOUND HOUND

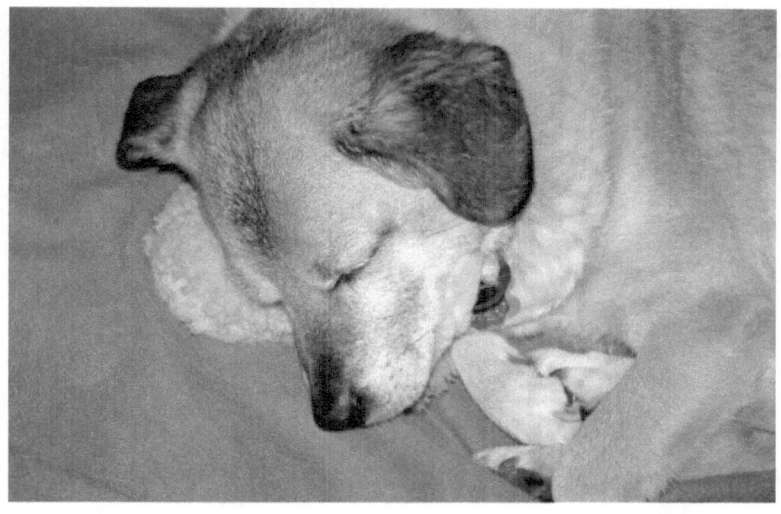

Shifting

Moments after I went to sleep, I awoke, floating. Below, I could see me—my head, legs, paws, trunk, and tail—lying listless and limp, on a table. Through my open mouth, my tongue drooped, extending far beyond where I ever would have allowed it to be.

Earlier, around the time the sun was high, I had hauled myself up the stairs slowly, groaning as my paws reached each step, determined to lay on the warm, worn carpet next to my human mom as she pretended to be engrossed in whatever words and pictures that filled her computer screen. It was an agonizing ascent but one I willed my aching hips to make. I didn't want to be alone. Upstairs, the scent of worry surrounding Mistress Carmen seemed more intense than usual. It stung my nose. I wished she could smell my fear and confusion.

We stared at each other, silently contemplating how much we both had aged since we had met. White strands framing my eyes and cascading down the slopes of my muzzle, like flecks of snow, also blanketed the crown of my head. Likewise, an expanding triangular grove of silver curls rose above Mistress' forehead and pointed back down at her right eye. The major difference: I was farther along on the continuum of life because infancy, youth, middle, and senior stages for dogs outpace the rate our human parents' age, seven times over. Such is the compressed nature of canine calendars. While Mistress moaned about turning 52, I was almost 80 in dog years. On the plus side, had our household followed a canine calendar, we could've celebrated more often—for it was criminal in my human mom's mind to let anyone's birthday come and go without giving presents she selected carefully, or preparing ambitious meals that were, sadly, often unsuccessful. A few of the latter involved cake mistakes, multiple ones with sunken middles we pretended to mourn when the cakes were devoured by the garbage disposal. If we had marked my birthdays, I would have lobbied for plush playthings and store-bought peanut butter treats.

Lately, though, I wasn't in the mood to lick, paw, or fetch even my favorite toys. And, the soft mound of food in my bowl may as well have been mulch. Air bounced around my throat and stomach. The last few times I had forced myself to nibble one or two mouthfuls of lamb and carrot mush, it had spent little time inside my tummy. Without fail, moments later, gooey half-digested blobs had erupted back up and out. Puking on the floor and carpet regularly was not pleasant for me and not easy for my humans to clean.

It was hardly a time I felt up to welcoming any guests, including my most beloved admirers. I usually saw my fans when I was out walking, not inside our house. But, into my living room bedside they came, one after another, reeking of a strange mixture of deep love and gloom. First, devoted human brother Brian arrived, then number one neighbor fan Sally, then next door friends Jack and Amy. Each one cooed and fussed over me, stroking, scratching, and rubbing my belly longer and more intensely than they normally did. Seeing them when I awoke from napping brightened my mood and made dealing with how miserable my tummy and the rest of my body felt a lot easier to take. The look on their faces, though, confused me. Despite their smiles, all my visitors had water in their eyes.

That was yesterday. I was upstairs now, lying on the carpet. As the sun started to sink, Mistress shut off the computer, signaling it was time for us to head down the stairs. Our descents were slow. Each of our sore legs pleaded for the next step to be the last.

Finally, my paws joined her feet on the cool, hardwood floor. Mistress paused, then grabbed her keys and my leash from the hook.

No, I just want to rest, my eyes begged.

She opened the door. I could hear cheery bird conversations and squirrels darting up and down the trees on the green space in front of us.

"We have to go."

Alongside Sam

On our last walk
You stepped slowly,
In stride with my limp,
An uneven pace,
Destined for where?

Down our long driveway
Unwilling limbs veered
In and out of grass;
Tail wagging in spurts,
Nose poking known spots.

Up your head tilted,
Weary and wary,
How far will we go?
I paused not to answer,
"As far as we can."

Heading for home,
I crouched down slightly
To stroke your soft ears,
And wipe your brown eyes,
Tearing like mine.

-Carmen Ambrosio

Off

Master Larry's scent seeping through a tiny gap at the base of the entryway roused me from sleep. He was home early.

When he stepped inside, I raised my muzzle slowly, hoping he would forgive me for not running to greet him as usual. I didn't have the energy to lift one paw, much less four. Even my tail lay motionless—a first for me. I felt as exhausted as Master smelled and looked. He walked toward me, frowned, and then sighed so deeply it sounded like he was releasing at once all the air he had inhaled since birth.

He headed for the bedroom to shed his suit and tie. When he returned in tee-shirt, jeans, and sneakers, he clicked on my leash and coaxed me to follow him to the garage. Usually,

I would have been excited to go outside for a third walk. Not that day. He opened the car door and signaled for me to get in. Mistress was seated in front on the side with no wheel. It really hurt for me to hop onto the backseat, but I did. I knew riding meant I wouldn't have to use my legs for a while. Traveling by the car was my least favorite way of exploring outdoors. Why should I sit down and be moved to places I didn't choose when I could strut on grass, asphalt, or concrete and allow my nose (and sometimes Master) to decide our path and destination?

So much had changed in those past few days. I had begun to crave nap time on my beds, not lap time, because of my stiff hips and aching legs. My ability to leap onto the couch had diminished to equal Mistress's rare and pitiful, barely-above-the-floor hops. Any thoughts of me springing onto the vast, comfy expanse of my humans' beds—sites worthy of a privileged pooch like me—were foolish and rejected. To add to my misery, the fur on my neck and back was riddled with tiny, tender bumps that made getting brushed and combed agonizing. Each day I ate, belched, and pooped less, and vomited more.

The car stopped. I knew the scents and scenery. I should've guessed where we had been headed.

We had arrived at the vet.

Inside, the nice lady who always sat behind the front desk welcomed us into the empty waiting room. I caught whiffs of three cats, four dogs, and their humans who had stopped by recently.

We took seats near the windows—chairs for Mistress and Master, the floor for me. As usual, being at the vet made me panic like a dog hearing the doorbell right after digging a hole in a couch to retrieve a non-existent pile of pepperoni. Mistress and Master stroked my back and sides to try to calm me. Their efforts were well-intentioned but hardly effective. I sat down and stood up, again and again as I glanced at my human parents' faces. The air in the front room, just like our car, was heavy and bitter with the odor of melancholy. But, why? It couldn't be because the sun was saying good-bye. That happened every day.

I continued to fidget, covering the floor around me with clumps of my hair before my dear doggy doctor came in and murmured, "Hi, Samson." It was not her usual, bubbly greeting. Then, she led us to a small room with no windows. It was not the regular, exam space.

She closed the door, wrapped her arms around my chest in a gentle hug, and lifted me onto a table. I turned and nestled my nose under her chin. I had to thank her in advance. I knew she could, and would, fix my tummy.

Yes, that's it. Everyone, especially me, will feel happy if you just rub my belly like . . . . Human mom and dad, why do you smell and look so sad and scared? I'll be okay.

I had hoped it wouldn't be one of those visits when the three of us arrived together, my human parents left, and I stayed in one of those wire jail cells barely bigger than me.

So, Doc, am I going to stay here with you overnight? Will I have time between whatever it is you need to do for me to meet some new pooch pals and ignore the whining cats?

She did not answer.

The vet unbuckled my collar and handed it to Master. He fingered the dried cow skin strap and sighed. A few of my neck hairs drifted to the floor. Some strands clung to his jeans. As my human parents sat facing me two steps away, I sniffed an odor I seldom noticed coming from either of them. Both were scared. And, shaking. I sensed each wanted to hold me. I wished one of them would.

Please, reach over and pull me near you.

They remained seated, wringing their hands and staring at me as the vet ran her fingers gently along the thick fur on my shoulders and back. The fear in the air got stronger.

Why did Master let Doc remove my collar? He knew I felt naked without it. The only time I was without my collar was when he planned to give me a bath. There we were at the vet, indoors, and not at home, outside, on our back deck. Plus, Master's lopsided flip flops, the dreaded water bucket, sickly sweet shampoo, and fraying towels reserved for bathing me were nowhere in sight.

Doc pulled me so close I could feel her heart thumping out of sync with mine as she stroked my ears. I was just beginning to relax and enjoy her pampering when I felt a sharp, shallow needle prick. Everyone gasped. Against my will, I closed my eyes and fell farther than sleep—plummeting down, down, down. I wasn't certain but I think the vet jabbed another needle into one of my front legs. I took a huge gulp of air and shuddered. I breathed out and my chest deflated as up, up, up, I felt myself rising, zig-zagging higher, quickly like those shiny rainbow birds with the superfast wings I only saw when the air was warm as they darted in and out of Mistress' flowerpots.

Near the ceiling, I hovered in a thin mist, unable to smell or see clearly. Sounds were muffled, too, fading in and out. I had to strain to hear. Was that Mistress and Master breathing deeply? Were they sobbing? The air around me swirled. Then, everything got quiet.

The sensations I felt made no sense. I had a dream like none I had experienced before. I was not chasing any ducks, rabbits, or squirrels. If I were awake and wasn't napping, why didn't my nose work? I couldn't smell. No air came in or went out of my snout anymore.

Somehow, I remained suspended above the humans seated below, outside my body. How could I be up, floating near the ceiling and me be down, resting on the table at the same time?

In the confusion, there were clear breaks in the haze where I could see Master and Mistress seated below. They were weeping, like I had seen them cry days before when they were on the phone with the vet. Now, there in the small office, they hugged each other tightly, struggling to contain the sorrow I could see, but I couldn't smell.

Somebody talk to me, the Sam up here!

I peered down from my bed of air and felt nothing. I wondered if my motionless body down on the table could. I tried to bark to let everyone know I was both below and above. Beneath me, I could see my pink tongue hanging long and low, fully exposed. Again, I attempted to bark. There was no sound from either Samson, floating or lying. Airborne Sam struggled to understand how I could think and see, but not much else functioned. Worst yet, I was a hound who could not smell— well, not well. Odors came and went. Two faint, uncomfortable scents wafted up and intensified. At first, I couldn't identify the smells, but I knew I disliked them. As the scents and muffled sounds grew stronger, I realized what they represented. Death and grief.

Doc asked my human mom and dad whether they wanted burial or cremation. I couldn't make out their answers. They were still sobbing.

The mist cleared again. The vet's assistant lifted my limp form from the table and moved my body into another room in the back. Through the walls, I could see her pressing the pads of one of my drooping feet into some pale, wet paste. It formed a paw print. Underneath, she added tiny a heart and S, A, M, S, O, and N beads.

"Go ahead. Take as much time as you need."

Was that the vet speaking?

I turned and gazed into the first room. The haze beneath rose, and enveloped me, distorting my view momentarily then cleared, like passing clouds. Mistress' and Master's voices shifted. Were those footsteps?

No, don't leave. I want to go with you. Come back!

I tried to bark again and failed. I had so much I wanted to say. Good-bye was not what I had in mind.

Move. I must move. Suddenly, I and my see-through air bed skimmed the ceiling lights, penetrated the walls of the vet's office, and emerged outside, over the parking lot, and into the vanishing afternoon light. I scanned the area from end to end. Master, Mistress, and our car were gone.

A gentle but firm force pulled me deeper into haze, across the sky. Looking down, I glimpsed rows of cars, streets, trees, buildings, and people. Somehow, I was moving without walking, running, or getting car sick. How? I'm a dog, not a bird.

All I wanted to do was to go home.

Reunion

Gliding high overhead, atop the same thin layer of fog, I could tell my location had changed. The smell of cars, concrete, asphalt, and burgers flowed upward. More noticeable were the aromas of recently mowed grass, dried goose turds, dog poop, and human sweat. My nose was working again. So were my eyes and ears. I peered at the field below. Kids were giggling and kicking a white ball much too big for me to fetch, as their parents cheered the children's hits and misses. What I would give to share such happy times with Mistress, Master, and my two-legged fans again.

I recognized the landscape beneath me—a wide, flat meadow with dirt mounds and nets bordered by a thick line of trees and bushes. Somehow I had moved away from the vet's office, dodging numerous treetops, fast food restaurants, houses, apartments, and a half-abandoned strip mall with more lights than customers and cars, to return to our old home, a few miles away. Here was the field where I used to walk and play. Across the narrow, dry stream and through a hole in the fence stood the multi-level house with many floors and lots of steps that used to be ours. There, to the right, on the hilltop rimming the ballfield, was the spot where, as a pup-teen, I remember rolling over and over again in an irresistible heap of sun-warmed fish. I was certain, at the time, one of the men who camped along the river had dumped the decaying treasure just to tempt me. Oh, to smell like a dog once more. I never under-stood why Mistress failed to share my enthusiasm for supremely stinky anything. Sadly, she never grasped that dog noses are broadband stenchometers equipped with sensors to steer us not only to tender delicacies like chicken, lamb, and beef but also to the most yucky, rotting piles of whatever. Mistress always wanted my fur to be perfumed and floral while I preferred my coat to be funky and foul. We had very different definitions of filth.

Look, there is the branch where the giant blue bird who

reeked of fish and frogs liked to land. I also could see the enormous tree outside the third floor bedroom where Master, Mistress, and I slept. While they snoozed, I would stay in vigilant watchdog mode, resting my nose on the chin-high window sill to monitor the ground and woods for trespassing animals or humans. A raccoon brood became frequent, determined thieves that enjoyed taunting me as they scampered up the tree trunk or emptied our bird feeders. Those ravenous bandits and I would eye each other some evenings for hours. Sometimes I would woof to alert my humans to the raccoons' presence. Sometimes I decided barking wasn't worth being yelled at.

During the summer, when our bedroom window was open, I used my sill post during the day to announce to any pooch pals crossing the field beyond the trees that I was stuck inside, and although I couldn't join them, we still could chat. A few of our human neighbors weren't as enthusiastic about our loud canine conversations.

Now, I was floating, off the ground, higher than I had ever seen the big bird and raccoons perch. Sitting or walking on the grass would've been my first choice, not gliding, up in the sky. Nevertheless, it was somewhat comforting to be so close to familiar turf.

Was I dreaming? How did I get here? I wanted to go home—not here to our first house, but back to our current home, the one where I'm sure Mistress and Master went after they left me at the vet's office.

The haze around and under me thickened, hiding the sights and sounds on the field below. The dense fog reminded me of the day Mistress and I had been walking. Without warning, the clouds sank, formed a blob, blocked the sun, and started chasing us. We hurried along the path, the one we took each morning and evening to and from our house, navigating the grass and dirt and rocks more by memory than by sight. Before we reached the edge of the field and the hole in the fence, the pursuit was over. We lost the race to the fog that day. This time, there had been no chase.

My body shook as the air around me chilled. Through the mist, four-legged forms floated by me in small, tall, mid-sized, plump, and scrawny shapes. I strained my eyes. The images became clearer. I could see the outlines of dogs of all sorts—from well-groomed purebreds to free-to-roam, seldom-brushed mutts—in the distance. They stood calmly, huddled in packs of four or more, drifting across the puffy landscape. I was normally pretty social, but since I didn't seem to be able to control my movements any longer, I couldn't steer my air bed toward the other dogs. I didn't know if they would welcome me anyway.

My cottony base continued cruising through the vast unfamiliar scenery driven by some means I couldn't see or feel or hear. Suddenly, I and my air bed, were still.

I tilted my head forward into the fog and focused my gaze. A towering shadow approached slowly and stopped. Seated on an adjacent island of dense haze was a dog with a gigantic snout that blocked the slivers of light above me. I flinched for a moment. Then, I sighed and smiled. The scent and massive shape were familiar.

Alfie? Alfie? Yes, it's Alfie. Alfie!

WOOF! the burly Golden Retriever form responded. In his prime, Alfie had been ninety-plus pounds of toffee-colored canine power no dog besides a cocky Mastiff, Pit Bull, or Rottweiler might dare to challenge. His intimidating physique and pleasant temperament also made him the perfect protector and playmate for a medium-sized, peace-loving mutt like me.

When we romped on the ballfields and riverbank years ago, I had admired Alfie's regal strut. It was a dignified style that fit a dog whose good-natured British human dad always wore a coat crammed with yummy treats that he doled out freely.

I bowed my head between my legs and arched my neck, the way Mistress had tried often, but failed frequently, to grasp, despite my repeated doga demonstrations and step by step instructions. Butt in air? Check. Legs and arms bent so your body forms a vee? Check. Toppling to the floor? No. [Sigh.] More than once, I had tried to explain to my inflexible human mom with baffling balance issues, that what she and her umpteen yoga books called Downward Dog was what canines call Hello Dog. It is the way pooches greet and invite each other to play. For those of us with paws, dew claws, and tails, we don't need fancy mats, skin-tight pants, and classes led by wiry instructors who probably are former dancers. Hello Dog is as ingrained in pooches at birth as pawing a spot then running around several times before plopping. We do it. We don't know why.

In any event, I realized Alfie and I were shadows of ourselves. He used to weigh almost two and a half times as much as me, and only if I jumped, could my head reach his. Now that we, and every dog around us, were mere wispy spirits, nodding, not bowing or nuzzling, would have to suffice as hello.

The afternoon's events—being injected, falling deeply asleep, leaving my body behind, floating, returning to the sky above the field, and reuniting with Alfie—confused me.

What is this place? I wondered.

The brawny Retriever cocked his head. *I'm not quite sure. Before I arrived here, I recall getting old had not been fun. It had become harder and harder for me to walk. My eyesight had gotten fuzzy. I visited the vet almost every week. Then, I remember him giving me an injection that made me sleep. As I dozed off, my mind and spirit drifted up, away from my body.*

Yeah, Alfie, I had a similar experience. I don't understand how you or I got here either. But, I'm so glad to see you.

Me, too, Samson. I've been gliding around for a while, groggy and weak. It took some time, but my ability to smell returned. I picked up your scent, and I followed it to you.

Amazing. I'm the scent hound, not you.

You should be grateful my nose works. Anyhow, this place is far different from the homes we knew. I haven't sniffed or seen any humans. And, I bet you don't feel hungry or thirsty. That's a good thing because I haven't found any food or water. Then again, I'm not craving either one. If there are any chew toys or tasty treats here, they are hidden., too And, yet, I feel rather calm and satisfied just being in the company of other dog spirits. Our souls after all, make us who we are. At least that's what my human dad used to say. He is a remarkable man. So wise. I think while our spirits are up here in the fog, our bodies are down there somewhere. I bet our bulky selves were buried under dirt or reduced to ashes and stored in a box or a jar on a shelf. That's where my housemate Dexter ended up. You remember him, don't you?

Sure. You two were always together. He was pretty fidgety, not calm like you.

He was an Australian Cattle Dog. And, yes, quite a restless fellow with a mischievous streak. He barely tolerated being leashed or led. Dexter's joy was all in the chase. Running at full speed made him happiest. He needed a purpose to feel useful. Sadly, we didn't live on a farm or own sheep for him to herd. Well, one day he went to the vet and never came back home— at least not whole. The weird thing is I smelled his scent once our human parents put a stone urn atop our bookcase at the bottom of the stairs. I heard them tell people inside the urn were Dexter's remains. I came to hate the word remains, Sam. To smell Dexter and not to be able to see or play with him was . . . . I missed him in our house and on my walks. I'm certain

Dexter's spirit is up here. Would you like to help me try to find him? Your sensitive nose coupled with my fetching skill would be a formidable combination.

I was flattered. But, as thrilled as I was to see Alfie and wanted to help him find his housemate, I missed my home and my Master and my Mistress.

Do you think our human moms and dads know we're here, Alfie?

I'm unsure.

Well, it's been a very long time since you and I romped together in the grass and hills near the river. When Mistress and Master decided to move, I didn't get the chance to say good-bye to you. Just as well. I don't like that word.

Now that we're together again, let's catch up. I want to tell you all about my adventures.

Who Found Whom

My human dad, Master Larry, thought his former wife found me wandering the streets. No, no, no. It was I who picked up her scent on the local dog devotee radar and positioned myself in her vicinity. When she spotted me, stopped, and invited me into her vehicle, I knew Phase One of my relocation plan had worked.

Her truck was roomy and filled with the distinct aroma of one massive dog, a not-so-puny one, and two young humans. Relief! The days I had spent desperately hungry, homeless, and lonely were behind me.

Thank you, Foster Mom Michelle. During the next few weeks, I bonded with her, her son Brian, and his sister as well as a goofy Golden Retriever (smaller than you, Alfie) named Bart, and a mouthy pooch about my size called Gabby. There also were three cats I nicknamed Sassy, Leery, and Scary, plus a screeching bird behind bars that tolerated my presence but wanted me to leave. Such wasted energy. I only intended to live there temporarily.

Phase Two of my plan meant convincing Foster Mom Michelle to let Master Larry take me to where he lived, his Ambrosio household, my ultimate destination. No lobbying, however, was needed.

You see, from the moment I met Master when he came to pick up my new human brother Brian and his sister, I had a psychic vibration I was the answer to Master's unpublished pet ad:

> WANTED:
>
> Medium-sized, non-drooling, loyal dog for home with many floors and rooms to roam and even more tall windows. Located near expansive outdoor play area with abundant smells, woodland critters, friendly pooches, and doting pet parents.

Just a moment, Sam. You want me to believe you orchestrated your adoption?

Yes, it was all my idea.

I applaud your ingenuity.

Engine? There was no engine.

Right. Why should I correct him? Alfie thought. Muddling words was part of what he found most charming about Sam.

Alfie, sometimes if you want something badly enough, it happens. You know, like when you are lying in the grass, dreaming about chasing a squirrel, and when you wake up, two or three squirrels run right by you. Slowly. Within reach.

Back to my story. I can't believe Carmen, Master's current wife, had been angling for a Shiba Inu, one of those cute but bull-headed, AKC-blessed breeds. One look at *moi*, Mr. Congeniality with my curly tail, and my new human mom (whom I called Mistress Carmen) retrieved her senses. Why would she or anyone else spend $1,200 to buy an aloof, demanding dog who probably would leave nag notes every day, demanding this or that, when she could adopt yours truly, an affectionate, appreciative, homeless mutt, for free? Okay, okay. Kind of free.

Master loved to remind me that my first vet visit bill was over $300. Poking, prodding, squeezing, and later . . . . Y'know, I'm still upset that no one ever asked me if I wanted to become a pin cushion *and* to lose key male, body parts. [Sigh.] The Big Snip ended my dating and mating life before it even began. No wonder fertile females I met later cringed if I tried to befriend them.

Anyway, during my first vet visit, I could've saved everyone (especially me) all the hassle of trying to remain upright on the loud, scary, cold, and slippery metal scale. I knew how much I weighed. It was about four times more than the disgruntled tabby whining in her mini wire jail, and maybe half of what the vocal, twitchy tan Golden Retriever I saw and heard in the waiting room weighed.

A few minutes after we arrived, I met one of my female vets and forever buddies as well as their cooing sidekicks. All my worry and torment were forgotten once Doc doled out some scrumptious, chewy treats. They tasted great compared with the dry, brittle biscuits offered in our household after dinner.

I'm sorry the excitement of meeting the doggy doctor led me to decorate the inside of our car on the way home. From that day on, Master, Mistress, and I learned that after any vet visit, ample paper towels and a halfway-home bathroom break were mandatory.

Thank goodness for easy-to-clean, dried cow skin seats.

Meet, Greet, Know, Keep

A Word from Mistress Carmen

Two years after Larry and I got married, we welcomed an addition to our family. Our adopted boy came named, thanks to Larry's ex-wife, their son Brian, and their daughter. They dubbed him with a moniker befitting a powerful, muscular, feared warrior. Samson greeted me in the kitchen, nose first, comma-shaped tail whipping the air more right than left, like a solo windshield wiper on high speed. The mixed breed dog before me appeared to be the offspring of an unplanned Beagle and Labrador retriever union. He had a tawny head that reached my knees. I guessed his weight to be about 40 pounds, probably leaner than he should have been.

I doubted Samson was as mighty a mutt as his name implied. He seemed more of a Sam or a Sammy than a Samson. We eyed each other with caution. His expression seemed to say, *I like what I smell and see.* I smiled. So did I. Content we had bonded at least telepathically, away he sauntered, his tail wagging right with rear-mounted, motorized joy to search and sniff the other rooms of our four-story home, upstairs and downstairs.

It had been years since my husband Larry or I had lived with a dog. We were rusty pet parents. Accommodating Samson's basic food, exercise, and bathroom needs meant reconfiguring our morning and evening routines. Any plans we made before or after work or on weekends thereafter would have to factor in Sam Time. Those adjustments were pretty simple. Remembering when I made a groggy bathroom trip at 3:00 a.m. that our four-legged roommate slept in his own bed on our bedroom floor, however, was another matter. More often than not, I would stumble. Sam would yelp. I would apologize. Sam would sigh and we both would try to go back to sleep.

Because he was a found dog, Samson's prior life and parentage were a mystery. He arrived with no identification tags, collar, or microchip. Then again, we were strangers to him, too. Our uneasy orientation as housemates spanned several weeks. When we told him, "This is your home. You'll always be fed," Sam spent his first nights with us supplementing kibbles he devoured from his new bowl with scraps he extracted surreptitiously from our kitchen garbage. Until he believed our promises, "Don't worry. We'll be back," he consumed the fringe off every throw rug we owned. Sam equated being left alone at home with the freedom to roam from room to room with us abandoning him. Years later, his separation anxiety resurfaced when we moved to another condo. There he sculpted new edges on the living room curtains to create an unobstructed vista so he could monitor the vast array of woodland critters scurrying in our suburban sliver of a backyard. Mutt communique received. Thereafter, we opened the curtains for Sam every morning.

During our initial months together, our found hound repeatedly reminded us that trust is earned, not presumed. His guarded response to our ardent overtures made us believe some other human(s) in his past had betrayed him. Nonetheless, Larry and I were determined to diminish his uneasiness.

Our efforts to reassure our new neurotic dog, however, proved futile repeatedly.

The Letters N, M, and S

Alfie, who knew nervousness could be the basis of a long-term relationship?

From the first time my schnoz sniffed her leg, I sensed my new human mom was abi-normal and stressed. We recognized in each other a kindred, nervous spirit.

The question was why? The sources of my worries were not mysteries. I had lots of reasons to be tense: I had a new home, new bowl, new leash, new food, new surroundings, and new admirers. I knew there would be new adversaries, too, but I tried not to spend a lot of time wondering who those enemies might be.

What were Mistress Carmen's sources of stress? She

didn't tell me—at least not out loud. She didn't have to. Being the perceptive pooch that I was, I could sense she had issues.

We differed on how our quirks showed. A few times, though, we dealt with things in the same way.

When I was anxious, I trembled, shed, bit my nails, chewed rugs, or barked.

When she was anxious, she nagged, bit her nails, or yelled.

When I was insecure, I followed her around, found places to hide, or snacked between meals.

When she was insecure, she called her friends, stayed awake, or ate lots of salty food (popcorn and other stuff she knew I wouldn't or shouldn't eat; I wished she would've craved bacon).

When I was moody, I stared at a wall or out a window, curled my tail around my head, or sang.

When she was moody, she laughed, yelled, or burst into tears.

I could go on, but I won't. I found out one reason she was weird. I heard her tell somebody she had Multiple Scare-a-tosis or MS. I guess using letters were easier and took less time to say. I don't know what it meant, but every time she said MS or Multiple Scare-a-tosis, she smelled both sad and mad.

At least he got Multiple as well as the M and the S right, Alfie thought. *The term is Multiple Sclerosis.* Not wanting to interrupt Sam in the middle of the story, Alfie clenched his teeth.

Luckily, I was, by birth, like those people she used to watch on the TV who told everybody whether it was wet or cold or warm or windy, a moodorologist. I could smell body weather, especially in the air around my human mom.

Alfie looked at Sam and sighed. *My dear friend, there is no such term. The humans who predict the weather, and do so solely for the outdoors, are called meteorologists.*

Really? That must be another one of your British English words. I thought meteors were flying rocks in the sky.

On with the story. My ultra-sensitive Beagle nose could forecast a bad Scare-a-tosis day. Those were the times I knew my human mom would be unhappy, flustered, and frustrated. If I had thumbs, I would have fetched the spray Master bought for such emotional emergencies and emptied the can so the whole house smelled like those purple flowers that calmed her down. During moments like that, I thought I should have called her Distress instead of Mistress.

I wished she would have accepted and not resented that I knew some things before she did. It pained my paws that she would get annoyed when I forecasted the onset of a certain monthly occurrence. I thought she would have appreciated not having to consult the calendar. I also wanted to provide a helpful heads up for everyone else in the household to brace themselves for the increased chance of her barking.

The medicine she kept in the refrigerator and jabbed into her legs every few days didn't ever make her smile. Needles were not my thing either, especially the long, frightening ones she used. I could deal with getting shots once a year, not once a week. Besides, the vet did my injections, not me. Sometimes not having thumbs is a plus.

If my human mom wasn't so hard-headed, she would've figured out after I joined the family that ample doses of Sam time would've been the free, natural, doggy remedy she needed. If she petted me more, she would've released happy hormones and land dolphins in my brain and hers.

Land dolphins? Alfie wondered. *I'm not familiar with that expression. Ah, I believe you're referring to endorphins. Endorphins. Repeat after me, Sam, endorphins. They have no connection to the sea or to dolphins. You scent hound chaps are keen on smelling things and vocalizing loudly but are horrid at pronouncing words.*

Buddy, I am fluent in Doglish, somewhat so in Regular English, and not at all in British English. Anyway, I think you can agree you super-affectionate Golden Retrievers are experts at producing endorphins. Endorphins.

Thank you. Proceed.

I learned to be alert and to keep a safe distance on the days when Mistress' hands didn't work and she dropped pens or papers or keys a lot. I thought thumbs were supposed to help with grip. Stuff falling around me was my cue to break into one of my original mutt melodies and invite her near me to cuddle.

Sometimes, when she put on my leash, as soon as we approached the front door, she would tell me, "Today, Sam, we're walking slowly and definitely not far."

No problem, I would shrug in reply.

Alfie, I knew you and my other pooch pals and fans would understand. I could catch up with you guys when Master and I went out later.

I often sensed her legs weren't working before she complained about them aching or being weak. All she would've had to do was to ask and I would've positioned my body against her legs to steady her. Even though my head barely reached her knees, I could've nudged her the way my doggy mom did when my newborn siblings and I took our first, shaky steps.

Hey, maybe that was the main problem with my human mom—not enough working legs or paws. Oh, well, at least I could've steered her to some comfy spot to flop if she had tripped and tumbled—something she did a lot.

I resisted every urge to shred those tall shoes she insisted on putting on her feet. From my floor view and given her lack of grace and stability, I knew high heels were good for her only to sit or stand still or to walk a few minutes max. [Sigh.] Logic never worked with that woman. After constant wobbling developed to sometimes falling, I was glad the day she followed my silent requests, donated most of her tall shoes, and bought ones that lowered her feet closer to my paw level. Wisdom and good sense finally beat pride and style.

I remembered another instance, the time the Scare-o-sis—Sclerosis—made Mistress more loopy and unsteady than usual. After several doctor visits, she stayed awake long after Master turned the lights off, yelled a lot at everybody and anything, and ate anything and everything. I even caught her eyeing the kibble in my food bowl. That's when I knew she had to be sick. Who would consider eating hard, dry dog food over moist, yummy delicacies inside our pantry and refrigerator?

Fate connected muttley me and my nervous mom. Most of the time, I was thrilled to be her abundant dose of furry sunshine. Being her Chief Cheerer Upper was one of my favorite jobs. Sometimes I made her explode into loud laughter, the joyous kind that made her tummy sore and her eyes rain happy tears. That made me glad.

I am proud, too, of getting her to follow me to our basement to practice doga (me) and yoga (her) while we chilled out to mellow tunes. The soothing sounds lulled me to sleep so fast I usually missed seeing her brave attempts to twist and fold her stiff body parts in ways I could easily. I loved those peaceful moments we spent together. I wished they happened more frequently.

I regret the many times my efforts to calm her didn't work at all.

It's Just a . . . .

Sunny, dry spring day. Out for my noon walk. I skirted the two, side-by-side soccer fields where you and I first met and we reunited, Alfie. Yes, the ones down there, where we loved to romp, next to the Orange Tangy River.

My, my, my. What an interesting way you have with words, Sam. The name of the river beneath us is pronounced Oh-len-tan-gee. Olentangy.

Thanks. Your human dad really taught you British and American English well. Plus, you speak Doglish. Three -ishes. As always, Alfie, I'm in awe.

Right. Please continue, Sam.

Safe, away from the yucky, muddy water, among the

low and high bushes over there, I was excited to explore on my own, leash-free. My human mom loped behind me.

URK! Suddenly, she stopped. Uh-oh! She scanned our surroundings, found a skinny tree branch and picked it up, ready to strike. It was brittle and hardly a sturdy weapon. Didn't matter. She raised the branch above her head, then swung, whacking the grass and ground one, two, three times. The puny stick snapped. She leapt backward. Her knees buckled. Somehow, the usual Madam Klutz managed to steady herself.

Curious, I walked toward the spot and tilted my head. I couldn't see any . . . . Hmmm. Mid-stride, I stopped. There it was. I looked down at it. Then, up at her face.

More frantic swings and more misses. Mistress was almost hysterical. I was not. Across the field, other human dads and moms and my dog buddies gawked at her, then at me, wondering what on earth the woman next to me was attacking.

I turned toward the people and pooches and gave a reassuring Sam nod. There was no need to worry.

For the offending *it* was thin, significantly shorter than me, and a quarter the width of my tail.

To Mistress, *it* was a legendary, scary, 23-foot, Ohio

anaconda. To me and the rest of the sane world, *it* was a garter snake and was wily enough to slip away intact.

Quite the tale. Pun intended, Alfie thought.

Tall Dogs and Tiny Things

Alfie and I wriggled on our haunches and pointed our muzzles down through a small gap in the haze. The kids' soccer game had ended. Children's squeals and their parents' cheers were replaced by barking and adults chatting. Several dogs and humans had arrived and were crisscrossing the field.

Do you smell or see any pooches you know, Alfie?

I don't believe I do. But, we're a bit high off the ground.

It's been so long since I was here. Even if we were lower down, I wouldn't know any of the dogs. I've got say, though, this place makes me nose allergic.

Excuse me, do you have allergies? Well, it is almost spring. We're way up here, though, amid spotty fog. All right,

49

I'll take a stab at deciphering that baffling phrase you uttered so confidently. Alfie closed his eyes. Concentration was crucial.

Take your time.

Aha! The correct word is nostalgic! Nose allergic? My word! Alfie shook his head and sighed. *I continue to be puzzled by your capacity to mangle some words and articulate others.*

Call it a special talent. We Beagle mutts are champion smellers not speakers. Get comfortable. I have another story. It happened on the field down there.

I caught a whiff of them before I saw them. Their bodies were brown like mine and lighter than you. Their four legs were long, wide near the butt and tail, and really skinny near the ground. Their ears were big and stood up. Their faces were narrow, like those scrawny, speedy hounds, and they acted just as jittery. They ate bushes and berries. Their poop looked kind of like the stinky, pellet piles geese leave behind.

I thought the tall dogs were rude because they didn't answer when I greeted them with a bark. In fact, the nervous nellies ran away. Why? I was half their size. Maybe, even with those big eyes, their sight was worse than mine. Couldn't they see there were many more of big them versus one medium me? They seemed to prefer the fields or woods and traveled alone, in pairs, or in a pack. They kept me under observation, like I was invading their turf. Then again, I suppose it was one of those what-came-first instances: chicken or egg, head or tail, leashed or unleashed? It didn't matter. When I got close enough to some of the mute, fellow four-legged ones, I realized they didn't have paws like me, you, or any dogs I knew. What they had was the most ginormous, pointed toenail I had ever seen at the end of each leg. Good luck finding clippers for those things!

Could they be some giant vegetarian dogs? But, what kind of dog doesn't eat meat? Because Mistress and Master had neglected to provide me with animal flashcards and seldom turned to the Animal Planet channel, I didn't discover that the tall dogs weren't our cousins until you schooled me. The not-dogs belonged to a different animal group whose name also started with the letter D, followed by E-E-R, DEER. Could've been E-I-E-I-O for all I cared. As you know, our language doesn't require knowing letters or spelling. Doglish is all about sounds, smells, movements, and expressions.

Alfie, I owe you a big, juicy, cow bone. You were the one who informed me that despite appearing tame and some-what standoffish, all big deer have brown belts in kicking and head butting. Your advice to avoid the males with pointy, bony branches on their heads because, when they're in a foul or frisky mood, they might feel the urge to spear or punt smaller creatures, was priceless. Obviously, an unarmed canine of my middling size couldn't, and shouldn't, mess with them. My barking and snarling might have discouraged the deer not to attack. Might. [Sigh.] I guess they didn't know what a mellow mutt I was. I wanted to meet and greet, not faceoff and fight.

It turned out it was best my nose and butt never got too close to any deer's front or back end. I found that out shortly after I joined the Ambrosio family. Master, Mistress, and I took a leisurely stroll through one of the enormous parks one car-sickness ride away. There was so much to see and smell in the grass and trees, hills, and fields. Together with my human mom and dad, I strolled happily along a paved trail, ignoring the deer we saw here and there in the meadows. Our mistake. Hidden in those deer hides were gangs of mini monsters content to find new homes on shrubs or animals.

When we exited the woods and headed back to the parking lot, Mistress bent down to pet me and saw one tiny red vampire, then another, then the whole troop, deployed throughout my fur. Luckily, the little buggers hadn't dropped down to my skin level. They weren't attached or sucking, and I wasn't moaning, barking, or howling—yet. Mistress and Master launched a frantic search-and-destroy mission combing over me with their fingers. My real comb and brush were at home. Our pleasant trip to the park had turned into near disaster.

Since that day, each month I had to get goop squirted between my shoulders to shield me from those dangerous blood-suckers the size of flies. I bet you did, too.

How ticks and fleas can pester dogs of all breeds, and make doggy moms and dads poorer, was something I never grasped.

Beagle Music

Prelude to
a Sam solo
signaled by
a snout rise,
and taut eyes;
as ears flop,
and jaws stretch.

The pose proud.

Begin a
familiar,
yet singular,
falsetto riff—
a warble
more yawn
than howl.

-Carmen Ambrosio

Wondering

Neither Alfie nor I knew how long we had been sitting on our cloud beds. The dogs, their pet parents, and the sun were gone. It was dark below. Light continued to fill the mist around Alfie and me. We reclined with our front paws stretched in front of us, still feeling no desire to sleep or eat.

I don't know if you've ever had a similar experience like the one I'm about to tell you.

I'll be certain to let you know after you've finished, Sam.

Just about everything was swaying back and forth: the ceiling, the walls, the table, my head, and my body. Everything except my legs. I was lying on some foreign, fur-free blanket inside a small jail—okay, a wire crate. The fabric floor and padding weren't as comfy or contoured to my butt as my beds or the human ones at home. I was, and wasn't, dreaming. It felt like I was sort of sleeping and barely smelling. I looked around, back and forth. In the blur before me, I could make out rows of bottles on shelves and snouts and whiskers behind bars.

Then, I picked up a familiar scent. Squinting, I could see a face I should know in the murky air. It belonged to a scent I recognized. Mistress? Yes!

Uh-oh! I picked up her I'm-not-happy smell. What's wrong? I thought.

Back and forth, my head moved even though I tried very hard to hold still.

Then, I heard Mistress shriek, "What did you do to my dog?! He looks like Stevie Wonder!"

The calm, smiling, young human who worked with my doggy doc said something about me not being ready yet.

"Okay, thank you."

Mistress looked at me again, sighed, paused, nodded, turned, and walked out the door.

Barely a hello and no good-bye. Wait, she's going to leave me here? The sun was falling. She showed up just to tease me? Come back. Let's go. Who is going to walk Master?

I bet she was abandoning me there because I always decorated her car seat whenever I rode with her. It wasn't my fault my tummy got unhappy and confused when I moved but my legs didn't. Did she ever think maybe it was the way she drove that was upsetting? Despite my usual urge to hurl while riding, I was considerate enough to aim downward, away from her seat, the dashboard, and the windows.

Focus, Samson, focus. Cabinet. Ceiling. Floor. Paws. Theirs. Mine. Back and forth, my head kept weaving, doing figure eights, the way my TV Beagle cousin Snoopy skated.

Then, I remembered something. That morning, after I had finished my breakfast and morning stroll, Mistress and Master had conned me into getting in the car. They said something about another "procedure". That is why I shuddered and shed whenever they opened the car door, long before they started driving. Why didn't they ever take me to the park with the ducks and geese? No, if I got in the car, it almost always meant we were off to the vet.

Being there usually began innocently enough, with Doc and her sidekicks cooing and petting me. But, that was followed by poking, prodding, and raising me on that loud, slippery up and down table to see if my gut and butt had expanded. Then, the dreaded clippers would come out. And, my humans wondered why I sang, squirmed, and squealed. What they called a toenail trim was a hacking!

A plump rabbit wandered within ten feet of my paws. I lunged at his rump and almost . . . . Oh, I must have drifted off. [Yawn.] Through a small window, I could see the sun was about to hide. My teeth felt smooth and minty fresh. My gums were a little sore. I hoped everything in my bowl that night would be soft. Perhaps, rice in a bit of chicken broth?

What happened after they forced me to sleep? Everyone knew but me.

The rabbit reappeared. I chased him through the grass and between the trees. I almost . . . . [Sniff.]

"Woof! Woof! Woof!"

Ah, she was back! Thank you, schnoz! She had my leash, too. All was about to be right in my world.

The crate door opened and I was freed.

"Woof! Woof! Wo—!"

Stop? Why?

I had to say so long to the other canines in my cell block. Plus, I wondered which one was named Stevie.

Indeed. Ah, the periodic, mildly unpleasant, teeth-

cleaning. I always tried to keep such excursions to the vet in perspective by reminding myself it always could be worse.

That's what Mistress said all the time, Alfie. I figured she stole that idea from somebody else.

Hardly.

Most Days Mutt Musts

Sam, thus far you've described some remarkable events.
I'm curious. What were your typical days like?

Well, usually, I had to:

Croon by the side of the bed to wake up Mistress.

(I filled in for the rooster we, thankfully, didn't have. If
I was up, Mistress should have been, too.)

Find different spots in different rooms to get some
Vitamin D.

(I wished the sun was more cooperative and stayed in
the same place.)

Bound downstairs to spin—paws up—and scratch my back.

(The basement carpet just felt better.)

Plop sideways on the stairs before Master put on my leash.

(I had to prepare myself mentally for each outdoor excursion.)

Pause, sniff, and pee every five feet on every bush, tree, post, or hydrant.

(Master called it a walk. Maybe that was his priority.)

Nudge every human I saw for some attention.

(Pets need constant petting. I was a pet. Besides, I always returned the love.)

Circle, pause, scratch, paw pat, paw pat—like a plane on approach waiting for tower clearance to land. Then, plop in a spot far from my original target.

(I had to assess the carpet's suppleness and depth for optimum napping. Sometimes, the initial area I chose was off by more than a few feet.)

Study my medi-tootsy-chewy on the floor before I chewed and swallowed it.
(Master used to get annoyed with me when my examination took too long.)

Park in front of my bowl for a few moments before I ate.
(No matter what they thought, I wasn't weird. I was meditating and hoping I would find a tasty surprise.)

When it was available, I had to devour fresh snow, like it was flavored with something other than ice and air.
(I preferred my water cold, pure, and from the sky. Plus, snow was fun to play in.)

Bark louder and louder to stop Mistress from singing atop the bike that didn't move.
(My floppy ears could block out only so much noise. She may have had fun. No one else did.)

Sleep on one of the beds, couches, corners, rugs, or stairs

for as many hours as I could.

(Master and Mistress thought that stuff was theirs. I let them keep that fantasy.)

K is for Kermit, not Klepto-

I guess my paws felt the urge to steal. Then again, the item technically was mine. Therefore, no theft had occurred and I was never charged.

Sounds a tad muddy, Sam.

Sorry, Alfie. I'll start from the beginning.

One day Mistress appointed (more like suckered) me into accepting yet another job. The woman seemed to think I needed less sleep and more to do. Somehow she equated pup with puppet, dog with gofer, and go-to, unpaid aide. I suppose those descriptions weren't entirely fair because she gave me food, walks, and shelter. I can't believe, though, she thought my appearance in yet another one of her creative projects wouldn't require some immediate reward. I insisted I be paid well for my time. What was my newest latest hound assignment? Creative Production Assistant.

Amy, our next door neighbor and doting Sam fan, had commissioned Mistress to create a custom greeting card for her brother-in-law's milestone birthday. The card was to feature a photo and an amusing story based on the brother-in-law's love of some frog named Kermit and other interests he had.

My human mom decided to write a mini mystery around the disappearance of the in-law's treasured, stuffed Kermit toy. Because my starring role as former-mob-snitch-turned-celebrated-dog-detective Sammy Da Nose required no barking, I had no script. My instructions were simple: lie down among the props. The story centered on my superior snout determining that the stolen frog was an inside job. In the tale, the scent of a tantalizing *GREENIES*™ treat (my absolute favorite food that, as a bonus, cleaned my teeth and breath) led me to a shallow spot in the brother-in-law's backyard. Inside the freshly dug hole was one of the treats along with the frog. It turns out the perps were the guy's pooches. When the dogs were questioned, they confessed. Their motive: pure jealousy. The man had been paying too much attention to his stuffed frog toy and not enough to his living, breathing, shedding dogs. It was a simple, cut-and-dried canine caper.

Mistress wanted to feature my picture on the front cover of the birthday card above the story. I welcomed the Doggy Detective publicity. For the backyard photo shoot, she positioned me in the grass and weeds beyond our deck in a spot so familiar she didn't need to direct me where to plop. At my nose level, were two books, some birthday candles, and Master's Sam Spade fedora that smelled like it had spent more time hosting spiders and dust than covering Master's head.

I accepted my role and settled my rump into our lawn among the props. Mistress played with her camera. Suddenly, two inches from my outstretched paws, she dropped a *GREENIES* treat. At the same time, a stocky figure rounded the fence dividing our condo units. Mistress gasped. It was a man in a dark blue uniform.

Cop not part of the setup, huh? I thought.

The officer said, "Hello. Just want to check things out."

Mistress sputtered, "I can explain . . . ." as she held the empty clasp at the end of a tie-out cable where my collar and I should have been tethered.

The officer turned to face Neighbor Amy and said,

"Thanks for showing me the place." Then, he turned and walked away.

None of us moved. After a few moments, Amy doubled over.

"You should've seen your face!" Amy mumbled. When she finally stopped laughing, she said the policeman had been there not because one of our neighbors had called to report me being outside and off-leash, but to view her condo. He was interested in buying it.

To be sure the cop was gone, my human mom walked around the side of building. Only then did she decide it was safe to start laughing, too.

The minute she surveyed our photo set and realized a key prop was missing, her laughter stopped and her face changed.

Uh-oh.

"Sam!"

I thought it best to act like I had not heard her. Instead, I concentrated on devouring the remaining *GREENIES* half, cradled between my paws.

How was I to know it was a prop? Why did she think I would wait until she stopped taking photos to devour a bonus helping of my weekly treat in the very place I loved to eat it, in the grass? Really!

Maybe it was because I hadn't barked when the policeman appeared. It's not like I hadn't smelled him before she saw him. I hadn't detected a threatening odor. Maybe it was because I was seated so far from the tie-out cable when the officer emerged she couldn't pretend I had been leashed, in violation of some city law. Maybe it was because I didn't even look up as I savored every tiny crumb of my prize.

Minor mutt mistakes. Nevertheless, that day I was demoted to Production Reduction Specialist.

Sharing

There were times when I would give Mistress a you-better-not-be-having-a-you-know-what-without-me look.

Surely, she knew the mere sound of tearing open the bag and releasing that tempting, scrumptious aroma would rouse me immediately from my deepest, squirrel-chasing slumber at our first home. Her excuses for sneaking downstairs in the middle of the night? To read or to do a crossword puzzle and escape listening to Master Larry and me as we competed for the Loudest Snorer in the Household award. Please! The neighbors, the birds, and the raccoons never complained about our noisy breathing. In Mistress' mind, she purred. Master and I snored.

Back to the snack issue. Why would Mistress try to

deprive me, her indispensable Muttley Muse, of one or two of our favorite delicious, crisp, yet supple, spicy discs of perfection? Well, my superb schnoz never let me down. One whiff of the bounty and I bounded down the stairs to join her faster than a starving coyote spotting a sleeping, overweight rabbit before she swallowed even one morsel. 'Twas time for sharing.

She knew how much I loved them. I savored every crumb—that is, until she ratted me out to the vet. Did Doc really need to know about my super special biscuit craving? Yeah. Yeah. Yeah. Diet. Schmiet. It's not like I indulged that often. That's okay. I forgave Mistress. I knew she only told Doc so she could keep the gingersnaps all to herself.

That's fine. She can munch on for both of us!

I'm fairly certain she has, Sam. I happened to favor peanut butter shortcakes and bacon cookies.

Ooh, bacon. You're making me drool, and I hardly ever slobbered.

Those cookies tasted absolutely sublime. Alfie took a deep breath. *Pardon me a moment or two while I savor that delightful memory.*

On My Bow Wow Trail

Another hole in the fog shelf appeared to the left. Gazing down through the gap, I could see two large, empty buildings with posts and no walls. Situated on one side were a swing, a slide, and a few picnic tables amid trees and grass. On the opposite side, beyond a rocky slope, was a river. Its surface was calm. The only humans around were men with thin poles taller than them, standing in the water up to their bellies. Along the riverbank, a pair of skinny white birds, hardly as tall, bright, or broad as the yellow one on TV, dipped their heads now and then into the water. I also could tell deer, squirrels, chipmunks, geese, raccoons, groundhogs, snakes, and skunks lived in this space. Their scents were everywhere.

This was familiar territory. It was the park where Mistress would bring me sometimes but only when the ground was dry. Stopping here was the least she could do after she disrupted my nap time for an unwelcome trip to the vet for a toenail trim. The green space below was much smaller than our hometown field. When Mistress and I came here, there wasn't much room for us to walk and very little happening to hold my interests. I was glad that our visits were short.

Suspended in the sky, Alfie and I sat in silence as we drifted, scanning the scenery below for movement. Trees swayed as the wind gusted. Our fog perch advanced forward then hung above the high cliff on the other side of the river.

Sam, do you know this place?

Yes, we are over the Sigh Oh Mo.

Pardon? No, no, no. I believe you are referring to the river known as the Sci-oh-toe. Scioto.

Fine. All I know is we're one long car ride away from the ballfield where you and I found each other earlier.

With that thought, I paused. If Alfie and I were above the Scioto, that also meant we were closer to my last home, the one where Master, Mistress, and I lived together. Home.

The more I had told Alfie about my life, the more our

air beds had moved. Somehow we had traveled without walking or running, or like we used to do in our car. Who was driving?

How do you know where we are?

It's near where we moved. What a confusing time. I could tell something was up but I wasn't sure what was happening. I knew there less food was going into the refrigerator, little to no cooking, and hardly any garbage. Plus, Mistress and Master spent a lot of time cleaning, painting, and hiding things in boxes.

Then, one of my recent fans who began visiting often, a lady who smelled of Rottweiler, came over and took the three of us on a car ride. To everyone's surprise, my tummy didn't get sick even though I had my usual anxiety attack on the way over there. When we had arrived at an empty house, I made the mistake of sitting down on the cool, wood floors. I had no idea Master, Mistress, and the Rottweiler lady would think my relief the drive was over meant I wanted to live there. Well, they did. In hindsight, I appreciate them considering my comfort and my feelings.

Days later, after my morning walk, two men who looked like they ate too little and another guy who clearly ate a whole lot showed up in a huge, loud truck. They loaded all the stuff from our first house—mountains of boxes plus our tables and chairs, sofas, beds, and books—and drove away. What could I do? Once Master put my food and my bowls into his car, I had to go, too.

Our new home had plusses and minuses. Most of the neighbors nearby were super friendly. There were more trees, just as many birds and critters, plus a pond close by. Another river, the Scioto, was a pretty long walk away from our house. I also noticed the local deer were fearless. They trespassed on my domain, close to our back deck, (they were bravest when I was inside) to devour seed the birds kicked out of the feeder. The deer also seemed to enjoy chowing down on our next door neighbors' flowers. Houses on the edge of our streets and behind ours were big. Paths for Master and me to walk were everywhere. All good.

What I disliked were the bangs and clangs that disturbed my prime napping times. The noise came from garbage trucks, motorcycles, mowers, and blowers during the day, and loud booms late at night. The explosions were the worst. They hurt my ears as much as the blasts made Mistress and several of my neighbor fans really mad. She called the huge booms fireworks and the people in the houses who set them off many, many words that sounded and smelled bad. No Doglish translation was required. When the fireworks went off long after we all had dinner and were getting ready for bed, I would nuzzle next to Mistress to try to calm both her and me down. Curling up worked for me. But, not for her. At least, I tried.

After we moved, it didn't take long for my human dad and me to settle into a two-walks-a-day routine. I looked forward to our outings with varying degrees of enthusiasm. Sometimes, when the weather was wet, walking was a real chore. Most of the time, I was grateful for the relief my walks allowed me. We usually took a turn around the place where we lived and then entered the park.

I did my best to avoid an overly friendly Husky-Retriever, a female many years younger and definitely spryer than me. She lived directly across from our place. From our first rump-sniff introduction, I knew all I wanted was an atomic relationship. She . . . .

I beg your pardon, dear Sam. If it only was friendship you desired and nothing more, the word is platonic.

Play-tonic, melodic, supersonic. Maybe a better word would be demonic. She cozied up to me all the time even though neither of us had any equipment you-know-where to do you-know-what. And, she was strong. Her way of hitting on me was to slam all 75 pounds of her body into mine.

Oh, poor Sam. Pursued by a determined vixen, a powerful warrior temptress.

Pure alpha female! Most of the time she refused to accept that I was too old and too slow for her. I wished she would have calmed down and laid down. Females!

Such the charmer. I trust your encounters with the other dogs were more agreeable.

Definitely.

On the day when Master didn't wear a suit and the big newspaper came, we took a much longer walk. I really liked those days. I got to visit a number of tall things, trees, and so forth. That allowed me to catch up on the comings and goings of other pooches who posted on the local dog blogs. It was fun to discover who had been passing through the area. I always tried to leave a little tail mail message of my own, although Master didn't always let me stop to read each and every one of the other dogs' notes on the trees and hydrants.

It also was fun because I got to see a bunch of my new buddies who lived in the neighborhood. Most of the time, the other dogs didn't seem to be able to leave their grass for a close sniff and some hound bonding. Often, though, they would speak to me as I passed. It always was good to hear from them:

"Arf! Arf! Bark! Arf!" (*Hey look, it's Sam!*)

"Bark! Bark! Bark?!" (*Hi Sam, how are you doing?*)

"WOOF! Barkety-Bark?!" (*Hey Sam, where are you going?*)

I felt special because I knew that I would be walking on, and they would be stuck at home. Too bad there wasn't a big field where we could gather and chase each other, like you and I did, Alfie.

Anyway, I sure hoped my doggy friends at least got a chance to go for a walk, too. Walks were something special.

Hound Healer

Once we moved our stuff into our new home, it didn't take long for me to become the neighborhood therapy dog. My mellow mutt, compassionate demeanor and silky fur made becoming my friend irresistible. Almost every male or female human I met—from already enthusiastic pooch fans to not-sure-I-like-wet-noses types—wanted to greet and pet me on my morning and afternoon walks.

Access to a lot more people at our new house meant greater chances for me to recruit admirers. I really appreciated the long and short massages my fans provided in the places I couldn't reach myself easily, like my shoulders and frequently overlooked butt region. Those gentle, finger scratches felt good to me and I'm pretty sure the rubdowns were nourishing for my human buddies, too. I responded by positioning my rump to warm a fan's foot, or I burst into a spontaneous, appreciative mutt melody.

As the Community Ambassadog of Happiness, I was serious about my responsibilities to turn frowns into smiles and brighten even the crankiest curmudgeon's foul mood.

My post was unofficial and my territory limited by choice. You see, I never felt the urge to pursue formal therapy or helper dog certification. As you know, there was a whopping difference between being of service and being in service. Certified service and official therapy dogs were my heroes. But, they worked. Being on the job for them meant focusing and attending to the needs of the one or more humans they assisted. The dogs who were recruited to do those jobs were extra perceptive and single-minded pooches. I was in a different league—too weak to resist temptations, and I admit, plain lazy.

More than anything else, I recognized how pointless it would have been for me to seek the blessing of any sanctioning group because of my aversion to obeying commands. I was far more receptive to polite requests or, if you will, suggestions. Responding to doggy barking? Of course. Obeying humans' barking orders? Usually, no. Besides, investigating squirrel, fowl, groundhog, and food smells preempted any other demands on my attention.

You know the difference between English and Doglish can be as wide as the time between the trees shedding leaves and growing new coats. I understood most human commands. Sometimes, I complied. Other times, I didn't want to be bothered, or I felt what was being asked of me was beneath a pooch of my unique parentage or priorities. For example, if Mistress or Master threw my stuffed jack and shouted, "Here, Sam. Fetch!" I might respond, why?

The only time I might have allowed myself to be subjected to strict training was if I had known there was an opening for a Weather Channel disaster therapy dog or an Armed Forces veteran buddy. Despite my shortcomings, I'm certain, I, The Sam, coulda been a real contenda.

Perhaps. You know what else is possible, Sam? I bet we'll find Dexter somewhere here in the mist helping to nurture a pack of brokenhearted dog spirits who were abandoned or abused by humans. Dexter wasn't just restless. He was a friendly, caring canine, too.

Sam Da Sage

Another Missive from Mistress Carmen

Sam may not have known English well (we suspect he barely comprehended Doglish), but he taught me the joy of going off leash and letting things go.

In the doggy world where four-legged life is condensed seven-fold, having a short-term memory is very advantageous. Samson demonstrated that as well as his unwillingness to fulfill his initial promotion from mere mutt to Creative Production Assistant during one of my home movie projects a few years ago. Oblivious to his duties on our bare basement set, Samson knocked over a rented video camera mounted on my tripod mid-scene.

Cha-ching! I thought, wincing.

I bent down and examined the dented camera housing and yelled, "Sam!" In response, he slinked away to a far corner with his tail tucked between his legs.

I fumed and imagined how unconvincingly lame my dog-did-it account would seem to the video equipment store manager. Perhaps, some stray Sam hairs protruding from a key camera part would bolster my dog-as-perp case. [Sigh.]

As I rehearsed my story of woe, something cold pressed on my leg. It was Da Nose of Sam. He had reemerged, and so had his tail which he was wagging enthusiastically. Muttspeak to English Translation: "Hi, how ya doin'?" Looking at his I'm-innocent eyes fixed on mine, my anger and exasperation quickly melted away.

To Samson, what he did five minutes ago was, well, five minutes ago. Done. Gone. Went. Besides, the felling of the camera was purely accidental.

When I returned the damaged video camera sans Samson hair, the amused store manager had pity on me. He charged me $200 to repair the camera instead of $600 to replace it.

Classic Canine Canon: Live in the present.

It's NWTBP (Not Worth the Blood Pressure, whatever "it" is).

Sam's #1 Rule and my new mantra: Let "it" go.

Canine Coach

Alfie, I'm sure you can relate to this next story. It's actually a letter I wrote to a certain human parent during my Ears Exhausted by Whining Woman Period.

Dear Misguided Mistress:

Why do you bother to read all those self-help books? For one thing, so many of them sound like they include the word "how", not "chow". Trust me, any advice written by so-called wise humans can be matched by me and other doggy gurus with paws and dew claws. I, in particular, work for cheap. You can pay me in food, water, walks, and treats— stuff you give me anyway.

In my role as your Personal Pooch Coach (a voluntary position I have assumed to save my sanity and yours), from my cozy perch atop our living room couch (the one you wrongly believe only is yours), I offer this candid, canine counsel:

1. Love no matter what.

It helps to forget slights fast. Did I growl when my weekly GREENIES chew arrived hours past my preferred noon treat time? No. Why? Because I love you. Plus, you can reach the box.

2. Make requests, not commands and demands.

My head placed on your lap, my eyes focused on yours, pleading earnestly and in silence, proved again and again to be much more effective than me barking. For the love of peanut butter, lamb, beef, and bacon, do not yell.

3. Heed Bod Mail™ to speed healing.

I know you know this one. I heard about Bod Mail™ in your first book. When your body speaks, listen. Feel sick? Throw up and eat grass or chicken. Feel tired? Lie down.

4. Use smell to identify the emotions of those around you and tailor your response accordingly.

If you had my superior sniffability, you, too, could detect both foods _and_ moods. That would be awesome because I'm hungry often and you have nine million moods.

5. Groom regularly to stay healthy.

I know you humans prefer showers to wet tongues. Dogs, however, don't need water or washcloths or towels or soap for regular cleanup. Do you still think humans are the more advanced species?

6. Find or create a peaceful place to relax.

I can sleep just about anywhere but I favor resting my rear on the third stair, your upstairs bed, or on the right side of the couch.

7. Focus on what makes you happy.

I should have made this number one because when you're in a sad or bad mood, I and everyone else, know to hide.

8. Even if it tastes good, if something makes you throw up, don't eat it again.

This becomes easy to remember when relief—grass for me, antacid for you—is in short supply, or if I'm alone and the front door is closed.

9. Make and appreciate friends.

Don't waste your energy or joy on mean people. They won't scratch your ears or rub your tummy to make you feel good.

10. Rest more, stress less.

Do not waste any opportunity to snooze. Humans spend way too much time doing stuff. Of course, this advice does not apply to things you need to do for, or with, me. By all means, get in the car, go to the store, and buy me more food and treats. I'll be waiting for you, asleep on the couch.

11. Make time for play time.

When you get old and your hips and shoulders get stiff, Old You will wish Young You had played more.

12. Embrace change.

I accepted moving from home to home, from unleashed to leashed, from grass to paved path. I draw the line, though, when it comes to my food. Messing with my menu is a change my gut and our carpet can do without.

13. Communicate. Be honest and vocal.

Toenail trim? Vet visit? Bath? "Woof no, woof no, woof no." Belly or butt scratch? "Woof sure."

14. Move your tail and the rest of you every day.

I walk to stay fit, do my business, and read tail mail. The city says Master (and rarely you) have to walk with me, hold my leash, watch me poop, and scoop it up, too. Talk about invasion of privacy.

15. Get outside and stay outside.

That's where the fresh air, fun, and interesting people are. Pretend you're a child again. When you were a kid, I bet you stayed inside only to eat, sleep, bathe, use the toilet, and drive your parents nuts. Besides, unlike me, you can open the door.

I closed my letter with, "Coach Sam has spoken. Now, be a dear and grab my leash. Let's practice numbers 14 and 15."

Sam, I find your insights to be quite bold, but nonetheless accurate. I imagine your human mother appreciated your candor. Did she heed any or all of your advice?

She was a tad hard-headed, like me. Coaching her was as much an everyday gig as her trying to get me to do anything without a biscuit bribe.

Kennel Confession

Before I tell you about the following episode at the kennel, dear doggy pal, I have two things to say. One: everybody has strengths and weaknesses. Two: I promised the Pooch Witness Protection Program never to the reveal the true identities of the dogs involved in this story for the sake of their safety, and well, mostly, mine. Trust me, Alfie, you'll understand why.

When I smelled and heard my human parents as they exited our car and approached along the gravel driveway, I rushed outside my kennel cubicle to greet them.

Hi, Master Larry, Mistress Carmen!

I'm sooooo glad you came back.

What have I been up to? Oh, sniffing, eating, peeing,

playing, sleeping, walking, and pooping. The usual. That's it. Kennel mom, tell them how much you love having me stay with you at Camp Woof. Yes, I love being here, too.

[Right tail wag, right tail wag.] "Woof, Woof, WOOF!"

Now, Mistress, let's go. Open the car door. Let's go. No! Aw, c'mon, Kennel Mom. Don't tell them about . . . .

Please! Allow me to tell what happened. Mistress, while you and Master were wherever you were, there were a couple of incidents here. Yes, they involved me. No, I didn't throw up in my room or anyone else's. Something else. Okay, okay, I'll get to it. First, yes, go pay. Collect my bed and bowl and leftover food. I'll go say good-bye to my buds, and when you, Master, and I are safely on our way, past the cows, horses, and rumbly part of the road, I'll tell you all about my week.

Uh-oh. Too late.

"Sam, how could you?" Mistress asked. "Harrumph. Get in."

[Smile.] Hope. [Wag, wag, wag, wag, wag, wag. Smile.] Hope. [Sigh.] Nope.

Oh well, now that we're on our way, let me begin. I was bored. That's it. Cookie had left for her morning walk. The elephant was there, alone in the grass. He looked lonely, like he needed a friend. Besides, having my bone pillow at the kennel, in my chamber, on my bed, full of my hair, and damp with my spit wasn't enough. I missed my first and favorite furry companion Elphie. So, I adopted Cookie's.

Oh, I should've asked for permission? Was I supposed to write a note? How? Remember, eight toes, two dew claws, no thumbs. Besides, I thought Cookie and I were cool. I assumed she wouldn't mind. She did. Females!

The loot was discovered. The elephant was returned. Sam was scolded. There was no perp walk, lineup, interrogation, indictment, or plea. Nope, the proceeding was expedient. Cut and dry. Open and shut. Plain vanilla. A crime of opportunity. A simple and imprudent one.

My pals Drake, Roscoe, Champ, Penelope, and Rusty had pointed their paws in my direction. That surely saved their butts. It skewered mine.

Okay, yeah, I said incidents. Plural.

Give me a moment. It is amazing how you, my dearest Mistress, can write yourself a note to not forget something and forget to read the note. But, you won't cut me some slack.

Anyway, by evening chow time, Cookie had forgiven me. I am grateful most dogs have the attention span of gnats.

The next day, I was restless. Who knew you would leave me at the kennel for so many sun ups and sun downs? I got tired of playing tail tag with my canine comrades. You know Camp Woof, my home away from home, sits along a rural road. Listening to the cows moan and the burro sound again and again like someone was depriving him of a vital organ was as entertaining as watching you pull weeds. Another diversion was needed. Snatching the rabbit was easy. All I had to do was wait. While Chester was tending to his evening business, I abducted and relocated the rabbit to my bunk.

When Chester came back, he wasn't happy. I pretended to be part of the fence. Poor choice. I forgot we dogs smell better than we can see. Luckily, Chester channeled his displeasure into barking, not biting.

Cache found. Rabbit rescued. Sam charged. Again.

For the rest of the week, the other dogs played with me. They did so out of pity and because dogs don't dwell on thefts that don't involve food. Nevertheless, I became the prime suspect in any other missing stuffed animal incidents.

At my hearing, Kennel Mom told me she wouldn't place me in solitary confinement if I showed genuine remorse and if I promised to refrain from any future bad behavior. Then, she commuted my sentence to lifelong community service. I licked her face. Kennel Mom also spared me by not adding an electronic monitor to my collar.

The end.

In your heart and mine, I'm no kennel felon. You certainly don't need to inform my neighbor fans or Big Red (Santa Man) about my minor indiscretions. Muttmas is coming and our home really could use a doggie door.

"Forget it, Sam," Mistress said. "Santa knows what I know."

Bummer.

And to think, Alfie, I forgave that woman more than once for cheating on me by playing with other dogs even though she came home reeking of evidence every time she did.

Misunderstanding

How many times did I have to remind Mistress that I was not to be disturbed for any reason when I was on one of my nine million breaks? Had I volunteered for two hours of front door duty? No. I thought I had been summoned to the entryway to soak up some Vitamin D and to warm myself when the afternoon sun began streaming inside. My presence in front of the storm door should not have implied that I had accepted the role of Security Sentinel.

Of course, while positioned there, I pledged to do my doggie best to monitor the perimeter of the condo. If I picked up the scent of something or somebody other than the humans who lived in our house, I promised to alert them as well as all of our neighbors within barking range.

Because door duty was quite exhausting, I did, from time to time, close my eyes. While I appeared to be asleep, I was, in fact, chasing an imaginary bunny or groundhog. Trust me, my nose was always on patrol. I wouldn't wish to miss the chance to inhale any yucky or bird odors wafting my way.

That I, a mere medium-sized, mixed-up Beagle mutt, could impersonate a canine of twice my heft with my ferocious, baritone bark was not in question. Therefore, I proposed that Mistress reposition my daytime bed from the living room to wherever she needed me to be. In return, I promised to be watchful for an unspecified, brief time. (My evening bed, on the floor, next to their big and impossible to reach human bed, never moved except to let the noisy vacuum monster invade my space.)

I had hoped sharing this information would prevent any future confusion about my watchdog responsibilities.

It didn't.

Scent-sational Memories

Samson, you make it seem like you and your Mistress were often at odds. Didn't you get your way occasionally?

Only sometimes. Not every minute.

You take entitlement to impossible heights.

They were privileged to have me as their pet, Alfie.

And you to have them, Sam.

True.

Here's another story. When the trees were bare and the sun disappeared earlier, I knew it was time for me to prepare for one of my favorite moments: Thank You for Cooking a Huge Fowl Day. Ah, I recall those delightful odors wafting from our kitchen. Yummy, yummy! Mistress would read my mind and open the door to the oven again and again until the air was dense with a delectable bouquet of basting bird. I only wished she would've given me a periodic, advance aroma alert—some signal to let me know if I had time for two or three snoozes before she freed the turkey from its chamber, even if its release was brief. I bet she was as relieved as me to see the fowl hadn't escaped or, horrors to all household nostrils or tummies, been burnt.

It was dismaying, though, to see her cramming dishes of extra stuff she knew I couldn't eat on the rack beneath our beautiful bird. Those other things interfered with the purity of my poultry inhalations.

My eyes would plead with her to move my daybed closer to the sacred roasting spot. But, just like when I begged for her to unlock the back door if it was raining or cold to let me enjoy my weekly *GREENIES* where all dogs know *GREENIES* should be devoured (yeah, outside in the grass), she coldly ignored me. I would ask: why, dear Mistress, why?

Oh, the anticipation I felt when she finally freed, then Master sliced and distributed, the golden mound of meat among human brother Brian, Mistress, and other guests. Moments later, I would scan my bowl and almost cry for mine contained not a wing, leg, thigh, breast, or bone. Let me tell you, such a blatant omission was equivalent to poultry punishment. I should've faked an upset belly earlier. Then, maybe she would've boiled me some chicken.

That's quite alright. Super scent-sational memories will fill my doggie dreams always.

For that outstanding treat, I thank her.

Something is Missing

Days after the turkey was eaten by everyone but me, the sun hid for so long that both my first and second walks of the day were in the dark. Thank goodness my nose steered me to each of my much-loved tail mail and bathroom spots outside.

Alfie, my friend, I don't know what happened where you lived, but at our place, that was the time I had to work really hard to get enough sleep. There was so much going on around me to disturb my rest: Master wrestling with, then hanging, string after string after string of lights (as if no one in our house couldn't see well enough already); yummy food smells (okay, those I didn't mind), and Mistress playing songs over and over and over again (that was absolute torture!). There was music with words, music without words, and tunes that were fast, slow, happy, and unhappy.

I begged for her to stop singing the moment she started. But, she never did. In fact, she mistook me to be her sole and enthusiastic backup singer. Instead of accompanying her in creating ear pain, what I really wanted to do was to chew through all of her holiday CDs. The only thing that stopped me was wondering how much my CD destruction might put future after-dinner biscuits at risk.

My biggest disappointment was when lots of my real and potential human fans came to our house and I couldn't greet any of them because I had been exiled to one of the upstairs rooms where I was ordered to remain silent. If only I could have reached the door knob . . . . No, I was sentenced to stay put and stare at Master's work papers I couldn't read and shouldn't ruin. I channeled my displeasure by defying Mistress' command not to get on the human bed in the room. Bah! I, The Sam, deserved elevation and comfort. In our old home, all of the windows were taller with low sills that served as ideal chin rests for prime sniffing, surveillance, listening, and shout-outs to you and the rest of our pooch pack. In our next home, I had to stretch my paws way over my head in order to reach the window sills. And, to get the best view of outside through the open curtains, I had to sit on the bed. Yes, the one I was forbidden to lie on.

To rebel, whenever I was confined upstairs, I would hop up (that bed was shorter than the one downstairs), plant my butt against the bed pillows to scan the perimeter below me, and monitor the squirrels, rabbits, and chipmunks running through in the grass and trees beyond the deck. Doing so quickly bored me. Starved for two-legged interaction, I would bark hellos and whine so loudly some guests downstairs would nag Mistress and Master to release me. Eventually, my fans' pleas would prevail, the door to my upstairs cell would be opened, and I would be freed to run down the steps. Then, I would give and take as much schmoozing from the adoring crowd as I could.

During one such agonizing Christmas imprisonment, as I waited forever for Mistress or Master to liberate me, I took the opportunity to paw another letter.

My Dearest Household Humans:

Okay, I've looked under the tree you put in the space where my daytime bed usually is and I am dismayed not to see any boxes with the name Samson on it.

I hope you realize your oversight is going to force me to bark loudly and regularly in Moose code (or whatever the word is) until I get some answers. All I asked for was one of those collar-mounted camera things so I could prove that I am not to blame for *every* hallway, rug, or mattress mess you find. Besides, I think it would be good for you two to see things in our home from my level. How would you like to have a noisy, moving, sucking machine near your schnoz or your paws? You're up there. I'm down here.

Anyway, please take a moment or two or four now to tell that Santa guy what a loyal, loving doggie I've been all year. I sincerely hope on the day you open your gifts and stay on the phone for way too long, ignoring I exist, I will discover a *GREENIES* chew or at least some kind of flavorful biscuit inside my WOOF stocking.

Merry Muttmas!

I surmise all of your requests, save the treat, were ignored, Sam.

Sadly, yes.

Choose Wisely

Weeks, months, years—time was way too difficult for me, The Sam, to understand. Maybe it was because I only could count to four. One, two, three, four paws. That was it. No abacus action happened where I walked. The big bird on public TV probably could have helped me learn more numbers—if I was interested in watching him and his fake fur and felt friends. I was not. I would rather have stared out the window to track the critters that trespassed through my outside space.

When my legs still had some zip, I had an unforgettable, sniffing incident I regretted dearly. The sun had just retired. Shadows were forming. I was lounging on our back deck, keeping my human parents and our house safe, when the scent of an unknown intruder jolted me into action. I shot off the deck, sidestepping Master's outstretched arms, and bounded into the trees. My investigation ended as soon as it began. I heard my name once or twice before I zoomed back onto the deck, my tail tucked between my legs in the yep-I-did-something-stupid position. I swiped my snout from side to side frantically, ignoring the threat of splinters and cuts to my nose. I was trying my best to remove the stink cloud clogging my nostrils and burning my eyes. Oh, how I failed.

At the same time, Mistress and Master yelled, *"SAM!"* not in a thanks-for-coming-back way, but more like WHAT-THE-HECK IS THAT SM—? OH-MY-GOD!

The trespasser had greeted me in silence. There was no bark, no yelp, no squeal, and no meow even though the creature moved like a ginormous wild feline. Was it one of neighborhood tomcat Socks' white and black, bushy-tailed relatives? No, no, no. No in so many ways. Had I experienced any clawing, hissing, or scratching? No! Had my usual butt sniff greeting been wise? No! Was my friendly curiosity welcomed? No!

Let me guess, Sam. Your inquisitiveness was rebuffed with a foul missile.

Whatever it was, it didn't miss.

Was it launched directly at your muzzle?

Yes!

Was the intruder's weapon of choice a swift nasty squirt?

Pooey? Yes! How did you—?

Logical speculation. You, my friend, came face to face with the sole creature feared by others, large and small, for his or her formidable, lingering odor arsenal: Monsieur or Madame ouf-ouf known also as Mr. or Mrs. Phew Phew.

Yeah. Why didn't you warn me about that beast? Anyway, my meeting with Phew-Phew was followed by six unscheduled baths, three boxes of carpet freshener emptied throughout the house, and five months of skunk funk in the fur around my eyes and my snout. Every time it rained, the stench returned almost at full strength.

Many months later, when my coat was finally clean, Mistress and Master forgave my butt-sniffing blunder on the condition that I would be more selective in any future rump greetings. Life lesson learned: leave les skunks alone.

The summer after the skunk left his mark on me, a neighborhood animal advisory must have been issued that I was spending more time inside than I was outside because a fat groundhog had the nerve to move in practically under my nose. Had we met, I would have warned the trespassing varmint to beware of the coyote. I saw him once before. He was about my size but looked and smelled mean.

You saw only one coyote? They usually travel in packs, and essentially are wild dogs. Groundhogs, by the way, are related to squirrels and other rodents.

Mean dogs and giant rats. Yuck! They're hardly any animals I want to see again, Alfie.

Ah, Spring

It had been some time since I had recorded anything in my diary.

You kept a journal? That is surprising and impressive.

The notes are all in my head. You know, it was me who inspired Mistress to write her first book. I hoped someday she would write one with me.

You meant for you. In any event, writing a book would be quite ambitious.

Not at all. I could do it. I just need her help. She has thumbs and knows how to type.

And, how to spell. Alfie paused. *Wait, how did you write those letters?*

Slowly and with my toenails. Writing took a long time and loads of energy. I had to nap after each page.

Indeed. Alfie shook his head. *I believe you were about to share another story. Please, continue.*

I had been preoccupied, trying to spend as much time as I could looking or walking outside. Master and Mistress had been kind enough to open the windows for me. That made my nose really happy. The good smells were back: grass, worms, flowers, and best of all, my two-legged fan club members out walking and ready to show their love of me, The Sam. Plus, I could hear a lot of familiar sounds. Sometimes, though, noise prevented me from getting the 20-odd hours of sleep an aging doggy like me needed. What the cardinals, sparrows, finches, robins, wrens, and blue jays had to sing about all day was beyond me. I wagged my tail. They chirped—loudly and way too often.

Earlier that week, the neighbor who mowed his grass ninety-five times a week was out cutting his lawn again, this time in the rain. I guess he missed mowing as much as we missed hearing no noise. I bet his two dogs wished they could find grass high enough to eat when their tummies weren't happy without getting zapped.

Trees and bushes separated our yard from his sacred turf. Something I couldn't see stopped his dogs from coming over to visit me. I wished someone had explained to me what it was. Maybe the dogs were scared to enter the woods. That was okay. They didn't sound or smell friendly.

Oh well, the humans who mowed our grass only showed up once a week unless it was raining really hard. Now, that made sense. I didn't like getting wet either.

Something's Up

I was up and out for my morning walk. As soon as I attempted to move, I realized my head and my legs were not speaking to each other. [Forward, stumble, shake, shake, stop.] My back left leg, in particular, was not in a good mood. I barked at the leg. Had I caught Mistress' Multiple Scare-o-sis?

Ahem.

Sorry, Alfie, Sclerosis. I barked some more. It seemed like the right thing to do.

Then again, I had heard Mistress say Sclerosis couldn't be caught. Something else was wrong. I knew that was true as soon as I tried to pee and poop, and though I strained and willed stuff to come out, little to nothing did. I stared at Master. There he stood, empty plastic bag ready to be filled, as my trembling rear-end produced nothing, again and again.

I gave up. We went back inside the house. Maybe I needed to eat more. I walked over to my bowl and nibbled a few bits before my stomach demanded I stop. Retreating to my daybed near the back door to sleep seemed like a better idea.

When Master returned from work, I had barely moved. I hoped once he shed his suit and tie and put on a tee shirt and shorts, he wouldn't grab my leash. But, he did. I stayed put. He called me to the front door. I rose and walked toward him slowly. Midway, I stopped.

Please, I don't want to go any farther.

He bent down and clipped the leash to my collar.

"C'mon, Sam."

I made it as far as the door mat and sat again. Master opened the door. Against my will, out we went. In the grass, beyond the front step, I barfed the little food left in my stomach. Then, I opened my mouth again and heaved. Nothing came out but air. I lifted my leg. Nothing. I went a few steps and tried once more. Drops of pee trickled out. I squatted. Runny poop dribbled no matter how hard I strained. That was it.

Master looked as dejected as I felt. All I wanted to do was to go back inside and lay down. My body wasn't happy. My human dad was sad, too.

The next morning, Master and Mistress thought I didn't know, but I was on to their shenanigans. They thought all I had were toes and no thumbs on my paws. Okay, that was true. But, I also had psychic radar.

I had a dream that I didn't especially like. In it, I sat on the back seat while our car moved past other vehicles and trees and buildings. I squirmed and shifted, trying to get comfortable, but I couldn't. I never enjoyed riding in the car. As the dream continued, I whined until my throat hurt and shed so much hair I hardly could see the seat beneath my rump. The car and all of us kept moving. How? None of us was walking or running.

Finally, Mistress opened the car door, and I hesitated before I wandered over to a familiar grass patch. I tried to pee. I looked over and recognized the building. We entered. I began shaking in terror. Oh no, we were at the vet!

Taste Matters

I hadn't been feeling well for a while.

At Doc's office, blood was stolen, tests were run, and a day later, results were reported over the phone.

The next thing I knew, we were on our way to a new vet. The building must have been in our neighborhood because we hadn't gone far enough for me to throw up in the car. I couldn't identify the tail mail I detected outside or inside the building from the dogs and cats who had been there before me.

The place was clean and bright and the people were nice. Mostly, I remember lots of needles and folks cooing then poking their fingers all over me. I didn't know the female doctor and her assistants. They stole more blood, ran more tests, and returned to the little exam room where we waited.

It sounded like the doc said kid-knees. I didn't know that word. It made no sense to me.

Kidneys. They make your urine. What you call pee.

Thanks. I wish we had lived closer together longer, Alfie, so you could have translated English to Doglish to me all the time.

Back to the story. Master and Mistress stank of fear and worry. They tried, but couldn't hide their feelings from me and my nose.

The vet spoke. My human parents listened, signed papers, rubbed my nose and back, said good-bye, got up, and left. The door closed behind them. I barked and whined, but they didn't return.

I stayed at that place for two sun hellos and two sun goodbyes. When the vet let me go home, I was a little sore, but glad. Soon, I started finding more and more of some small, cardboard-like pellets in my bowl, instead of my usual, delicious kibble. The new stuff was not food. It was tasteless!

During our time together, I had heard Mistress Carmen and Master Larry talk about not eating twigs and bark. I'm not sure why they even mentioned bark. That's what I did. And, yes, I was a dog, but I did not eat twigs—at least not by choice, not like our neighbor's female Labrador retriever who carried or gnawed on branches all the time.

Every morning I looked and sniffed my bowl. That awful stuff was always in there. I tried, but I couldn't eat those pellets. Soon I found out mutts cannot survive on water, one biscuit a day, and a weekly *GREENIES*. My humans and my belly became sad.

Then, thank my lucky paws, my buddy and Kennel Mom at Camp Woof, my home when my humans weren't home, suggested a yummy alternative. The food was in different bag, still looked like little stones, smelled better, and had great flavor.

The vet, my humans, and my tummy became happy. My appetite was back and I was right tail wagging again!

Grateful

As the sole hound in our household, I welcomed the attention showered on me. I had a crate filled with my giant jack stuffed toy, a soft boned-shaped pillow, Elphie, a rope pull, a tennis ball, and other playthings thanks mostly to Miss Kay. I'm sorry I never met her. Mistress said Miss Kay lived so far if we drove there I would shed so much I might be hairless by the time we reached her house. I knew she was a doting doggy mom because her caring scent and her dogs' odor were all over the big, box filled with goodies she sent for me right after I became an Ambrosio.

My food and water bowls were filled every morning. When the sun disappeared and it got dark outside, I dined on lamb, chicken, or beef kibbles and a biscuit. On the day of the big newspaper when Master and I went for a long walk, I got to enjoy a treat usually outside in the grass.

I often thought about all my dog buddies who had no house, no Masters or Mistresses, no doggie or human beds, no sofas, no treats, no leash or license, no doggie doctor . . . . When I was a pup-teen, I was without a home, too. I remember scrounging for food in garbage and lapping water in puddles wherever I could. Then, one day as I tried to dodge cars and trucks, Foster Mom rescued me from the road and made me a family pet. My tail has wagged just about every Muttley moment since.

Now that I think about it, Alfie, some of my old homeless pals may be here in the mist, too. I didn't get close enough to the dogs I saw when I arrived or to the ones we've passed to see if I recognized anyone. It would make me happy to know pooches who were bred and kept in puppy mills or abandoned or neglected or mistreated or lost are here and have formed new packs to heal their spirits, to feel safe, to love, and to be loved again.

Absolutely, Sam. I've never understood how some people can be so cruel and others so caring.

I know—especially since our needs are so simple. Feed us, walk us, play with us, keep us safe, and you'll have the happiest, loyalist, protectivist pooch ever.

Samson, you can't just add -ist to every word. But, I agree with you otherwise.

Every dog deserves love and belly rubs.

Absolutely. I sincerely hope any dog spirits up here who were scarred emotionally and physically from their time alive are regaining their ability to be trusting, loving, and forgiving thanks to being with new pooch pals. Companionship soothes and heals, my friend. Pack love is quite powerful.

That is worth a bunch of woofs, Alfie!

Musing

(Please forgive me while I indulge Mistress Carmen again. She feels the need to interrupt my stories with her own thoughts.)

Most of Samson's thick, velvety coat was the color of the gooey caramel in the middle of a candy bar. As he aged, the fur framing his eyes and nose grayed, struggling to keep pace with his master's growing salt, and waning pepper, mane.

We loved Sam because he was a unique, blended breed. He sang and barked like a Beagle, ran like a Pembroke Welsh Corgi, tracked scents like a Coonhound, and befriended everyone like a Retriever. Once, on a walk, he stopped, arched a front leg like a Pointer, and then turned to me as if to ask, *why did I do that?*

I thought, *because you're—hell, if I know. Confused. Yes.*

In the eighth year after Sam adopted us, I struggled to accept he was slowing down. Gone, though, were the days he would race to greet us whenever we returned home. In the kitchen, rows of prescription and supplement bottles (to prevent or alleviate this or that illness or ache) bore his or one of our names. The household calendar became more crowded with doctor appointments, mostly for him. All of us were aging and graying, while trying to deny both were happening.

It was a time when Sam relished being home alone for hours, comfortably ensconced on the living room sofa beneath a thick crocheted family heirloom afghan to warm his arthritic body and hips. It seemed to truly annoy our beloved 80-dog-year-old mutt to hear the garage opening or a key unlocking the front door. When he heard either sound, he would raise his head sluggishly from the sofa arm in utter disgust that we had the audacity to return home before he cared to relinquish his comfy throne.

Fortunately, Sam's discontent, like most of his moods, would not last. Maybe, like the humans in our household, it was because he just couldn't recall what, or why, he had been doing something.

One thing that remained unchanged was the way Sam felt

obligated to let out a booming bark at the sound of a doorbell or knock, regardless of the source—front door or TV—and our proximity to him. Unbeknownst to circumspect delivery drivers and visitors, familiar and not, opening the door was Sam's cue to stop barking loudly, *Who are you? What do you want?* and start right tail wagging and woofing, *Hi! How ya doin'?*

Mistaken Identity

Mistress knew my name was Samson, although I did respond to other versions. She also was aware I was a confused breed. Sure, my superior smelling talents would have qualified me to be grouped with those snooty scent hounds, if one overlooked my unknown pedigree and non-existent birth certificate. No DNA test ever was conducted to determine whether my mama or papa was a Beagle, a Corgi, a Retriever or, heavens forbid, a Chow Chow. I didn't dig. I chased small varmints in my youth. I weighed around 48 pounds. I played fetch when I felt like doing that.

My origins were never an issue in the Ambrosio home

until one sunny, summer day when Mistress fell in our back-yard. In my defense, I did what my doggy brain told me to do. Instinctively, I laid down beside my human mom.

That act, I soon discovered, was insufficient. That I did not decide to bark, run, and somehow summon some other human passing by as the crucial tasks I ought to undertake was, I believe, too much to ask of a mutt of my ancestry. Instead, I offered Mistress warmth, sympathy, and a comforting paw pat in the grass as she massaged her right ankle.

I was pleased. She was not. I didn't know why. It wasn't often that she and I got to bond down at my level. When we did, it usually was while we were inside and on the carpet. Grass was a far more superior and natural surface. Anyway, my name was not Lassie or Rin Tin Whoever. It was Sam. It still is.

Afoul

Sam, stop!

What?

Stop talking. Please. Just for a moment, I want to savor this spectacle. Look, overhead, an undulating stream of chatty starlings is approaching. See how they blanket the air. There must be hundreds of the speckled birds, skittering past then doubling back, to weave, divide, and regroup in precisely synchronized acrobatic maneuvers.

Alfie, why do you care about those birds? They are fatter than sparrows and cocky like blue jays. Plus, it's not as if we haven't seen them before. One or two stragglers used to show up at our bird feeders all the time. I figured they had lost the flock flight plan or maybe they just had gone rogue.

Perhaps. But, now that you and I aren't relegated to observing the starlings from the ground, I want to enjoy their magnificent performance from our cloud perch. I find their movements absolutely mesmerizing!

There was an advantage to our spirits being in the sky. We were traveling without walking or running. And, we weren't getting tired, hungry, or thirsty.

The flock made one final swoop, and sped toward the disappearing sun, as if Alfie and I were not moving. But, we were. I could tell we had floated over land, away from the Scioto River because beneath us I could see many tall and wide houses, a small stream, large lawns, and pond after pond.

I was glad the birds had flown away, screaming as they left. They must have panicked when they spotted the huge hawk perched atop a giant oak at the edge of the woods ahead. It looked like the hawk was considering whether to dine on a starling or stay put and relax. He must've been full because he didn't move.

Only the starlings knew where they were headed next. Who knew where we were going?

The birds and the landscape below made me remember

something else.

I have a bird story for you, Alfie.

I expected as much. Go on, please.

Mistress and I went strolling on a not so chilly morning, long after the sun came up. My neighbor fans and pooch pals must've been inside or somewhere else. Only the squirrels were scampering around, losing their minds. For me, it was kind of a boring walk—until . . . .

As I made my usual turn at the top of a hill, my super sniffer picked up something. Nose up! Could it be? Why, yes, I knew the smell. Just to be sure, I did what any renowned Doggy Detective would do. I stuck my head in a low, all-green bush to investigate. But, before I could get a good whiff, a brown blob shot out and whizzed by my head.

"Ahhhh!" My mistress wobbled and almost fell over. "Duck?!"

There was a lot of angry squawking and loose feathers flying.

Okay, I hadn't expected that either. We were nowhere near the pond.

The duck mama squawked again, then turned, and waddled back inside the bush. Assault over. Case closed.

I strutted away. Mistress followed slowly, reeking of annoyance.

How could my schnoz resist the smell of live fowl?

Tempting, indeed, Sam. I preferred my poultry larger, seasoned, and roasted.

Road Trip (Off to . . . .)

Here is a story that's worth sharing not for what happened, but for what didn't happen.

I had downed my breakfast and medi-tootsy-chewy then settled onto my daybed overlooking my backyard domain only to be interrupted by . . . .

"Come here, Sam." It was Mistress. She had her sneakers on and my leash in her hand.

Great! A bonus walk! Despite my achy legs, I wanted to be outside.

She opened the door to the garage and grabbed something off a shelf.

Yes, get some poop bags. I'm ready. There you go reading my mind again. You and me off to greet my neighbor fans, dog buddies, plump rabbits . . . . Let's see if we can spook the lazy frogs and irk the turtle.

Then, she pushed the button. Light poured inside.

Why are you . . . ?

"C'mon, Sam." Then, she opened the car door. "In."

What? [Sigh.]

In the interest of receiving my after-dinner biscuit later, I hopped onto the car seat.

As the car backed away, I steadied my butt and turned to face her. Please. We're not going to the vet, right? We went last week. I don't need any more medi-goop. And, look, my nails haven't grown.

Near the end of the driveway, she turned right.

I pleaded with my eyes. Don't head toward the special kid-knees vet.

She drove away from the sun, around the road circle, the way I chased my tail. I had no idea where we were going.

Mistress made more turns and stops and starts. I tried not to shake or shed as the car shook on the bumpy ground. It was hard to stay upright. The road smoothed again. We veered right. She turned off the car. Before us, I saw lots of dirt and fences.

What is this place?

"We're at the new dog park," she said.

Really? Dog singular or plural? Unless you are dreaming (I'm pretty sure I'm not), there aren't any other pooches here. Run around? Why? You've got to be kidding! There is no one to meet, no butts to smell, no trees or bushes marked with tail mail. Just mud and more mud, you and me. Play? Hey, don't toss my stuffed jack into that muck! Okay, okay. Because you brought bags, the least I can do is to fertilize the area. The place definitely needs some grass and trees.

Mistress reeked of disappointment and sadness. She looked down at me and out at the empty park. Then, she shut her eyes, put her head down, and frowned.

Please don't be upset, I thought. You didn't know there wouldn't be any other dogs here. Did you? C'mon, let's head home, put away the car, and walk to the pond. That's where the action is.

Moving On

In the haze, Alfie and I had passed packs of puppies and middle-aged dogs romping while senior dogs lounged, clustered along the edges, content to swap life stories, like the older humans Master told me about who meet at diners for breakfast and coffee, or gather in parks to play chess and dominoes.

Below, I saw the dense woods where Master and I had walked near but never entered because of the deep ditches there. He didn't want to risk breaking his legs or mine. Beyond the pine, oak, walnut and ash trees, the lawns, bushes, fire hydrants, and walkways still held my scent. These were the places I had visited and marked, day after day, year after year. Alfie and I were close to where I wanted to be. I wished I could steer our cloud platform. Thankfully, we continued in the right direction.

Sam, I am convinced Dexter must be here among the other dogs in the mist. What does your olfactory sense tell you?

I don't have an old factory.

I wasn't suggesting anything of the sort. Olfactory means smelling ability. Look, if you can direct me to Dexter, I would be ever so grateful. Working together, we would make a fine search team.

I was flattered. Alfie had listened to me patiently relive the highlights of my life as we traveled side by side through the haze. It was my turn to do something equally special for my best pal.

Sure, I will help you, Alfie. But, there is one thing I must do. Alone. Wait here, please.

Before he could answer, the space between us widened quickly, then separated.

I'll come back. I promise.

My air bed shifted again. The farther away I moved, the smaller Alfie and his bed became. Underneath me, rows and rows of look-alike houses appeared again. It was the time of year when humans and animals began spending more time out-side than inside. The days and weeks of waiting for bare trees to blossom and the air to warm were almost over. Along the many sidewalks and streets crisscrossing neighborhood after neighborhood, people strolled or jogged in pairs or solo, some with dogs on leashes or babies in strollers. They were headed toward, or away from, a park and pond on the other side of the woods.

Alfie would've been amused by the cardinals, blue jays and other birds trying to find mates as they perched on branches and competed for seed at feeders, outnumbered by busy-body sparrows. It wouldn't be long before pairs would scout roofs and trees and ready-made houses hung by humans for suitable places to build nests.

Just over a small hill, at the end of a path leading away from the park, I recognized the bricked entryway and the long driveway winding through and around wide, grassy areas in the middle of tall, attached buildings.

The car parked in Master's spot looked unfamiliar but held his scent. I lowered myself below the adjacent roof's edge and sampled the air again. Mistress had been outside recently, probably to get the mail. Near the front door, I paused. A tile with the paw print of some gigantic dog and some letters had been added under the outdoor light on the wall.

Inside, I could hear my human parents talking. I entered the house through the closed front door, breaching the surface easily. I positioned myself by the ceiling, just inside the upper bank of windows that flooded the room with the light of the sun or the moon. They were seated at the dining room table, eating salmon, food I disliked but any cat would crave.

Since Master, Mistress, and I had parted at the vet, what had the two of them been doing and with whom? Did Master walk every morning and evening anymore? Whose furry ears and back did Mistress massage? Who planted their rump on the third step and crooned a doggie song? Who devoured *GREEN-IES* in the grass on the day of the big newspaper and begged for lap time every night?

I woofed. Neither my human mom nor dad looked up.

"Jeopardy" was on—as it usually was during dinner. Determined to get their attention away from whatever clue Alex Trebek was reading, I descended, hovered above the kitchen counter, almost level with their heads, and woofed again.

Forget the fish and the TV. Can't you hear me?

"The house is so empty without him," Master said.

Mistress put down her fork, frowned, and nodded.

Hey, I'm right next to you. I know you can't smell me, but can't you see me?

I guessed not. Perhaps it was best they couldn't for I didn't want to frighten them. To my human parents and other two-legged fans, the Samson they knew was dead. I wished I could tell them the truth. My spirit had survived.

They finished their dinner to the sounds of Trebek's final question and the contestants' answers. Master collected the emptied plates and began rinsing and loading them into the dishwasher. Mistress limped to the drawer where she stowed the placemats, then retreated to the sofa. Master's hair seemed grayer and longer. Mistress' was curlier and shorter. Had I been traveling that long?

I pivoted to scan the area. To my left, on the hook next to the door to the garage, hung my leash with my license and vaccine tags attached. Across the room, Elfie and my stuffed toy jack stood guard behind the tall, always-green leaves-but-never-any-flowers-plant in the wide pot next to the back door. The spot where my daybed used to be, to the left of the never-used fireplace, was empty. So was the corner of the floor under the kitchen counter. My food and water bowls were gone.

I inhaled again. The strong salmon smell did not mask the deep sorrow filling the air around my human parents. Their unhappiness made me sad, too. In this place where I had lived and slept and played and ate, evidence of me remained. My odor was still on the furniture, carpet, and floors.

I was comforted by one thing. I was home. Home, back in a different form, but back again. Aboard a cloud platform, transported somehow through the mist by memories and the intense wish to return to Master and Mistress, I had found my way home.

I glanced to the right. On the wall close to the TV cabinet, I saw a picture where none had been before. It was Mistress' favorite photograph of me. I really liked that one, too. For once, when she had pointed her camera at me, I had cooperated long enough for her to capture my noble muttness, head held high in a dignified pose, under the light of two table lamps. She knew I disliked having my picture taken almost as much as I hated swallowing pills. The evening she took the picture no biscuit bribe had been necessary to get me to sit still. I had felt too ill and weak to protest.

I stared at the photograph. How weird it was to see myself again in the fur and flesh. Below the image, in the same wooden frame, was the tile imprint the vet's assistant had cre-ated with one of my paws after my body went limp and my spirit became airborne.

It was then I noticed something else. There was no sign of a new dog.

I knew what I had to do next.

Hunt

Thanks to Mistress, I had held many jobs over the years in our Ambrosio household including Lap Warmer Upper, Not-so-Clandestine Couch Sitter, Downward Dog Doga Authority, and Ground-level Rover Reporter. Seeing and smelling how sad my human mom and dad were after I moved into the sky inspired me to take on yet another post—Replacement Dog Recruiter.

No pooch was more qualified than me to locate and approve a new dog for Mistress and Master to spoil. I began to draft my ad for the local All Paws Network:

Seeking family dog

Male or female (doesn't matter)

Breed not that important, though mutts and non-droolers will be given special consideration

Absolutely no biters or fighters

Pup-teen or older (Sorry, Mistress and Master don't have the energy, time, patience, or paychecks to care for a puppy)

About 50 pounds (although I know Master would prefer to have a big Retriever like Alfie or a Burned-knees Mountain Dog, the brown and black ones with ginormous paws and a go-to-the-store-everyday appetite)

Laid back

Patient

Trusting of humans and can be trusted not to destroy the house when left alone

Loyal

Loving

Makes friends easily

Knows the doggy bathroom is just about anywhere outside and nowhere inside

Chews only food and stuffed toys and not shoes, pillows, papers, furniture, cushions, fingers, or legs

Finds joy digging in a stuffed toy box and not in flowers or dirt

Able to keep up on walks with Master Larry a.k.a. Legs of Steel and slow down for Mistress Carmen

Will be supplied with ample food, treats, water, walks, beds, belly rubs, toys, and lap time

That's done. The key will be for Master and Mistress to think the new dog they adopt is their idea. My search must be done out of sight. That will be easy now that I know, even when I'm right in front of them, they can't see me.

But, before I leave the house, there is one more thing. Actually, two.

Always Close

Dear Mistress and Master:

I pawed through your piles of photos to find another one of me you took with some of my favorite things.

Without any cues from you, notice how I had positioned my stuffed bone pillow and gnawed jack (intentionally moistened to repel human hands) carefully atop my daytime bed for easy access and necessary napping. Although I miss these things, I miss both of you more.

Guess what? I wrote a poem for you. It is not my finest verse. Mistress, please forgive me for not taking days and days to obsess over how the words flow, like you often did. Time always confused me, and since we parted at the vet, the number of sun ups and downs is fuzzy. This poem is purely off-the-paw and a bit rushed

157

because Alfie is waiting for me. Yes, we've found each other again. I promise to share details of our reunion and our travels with you sometime soon. In the meantime, know that what I wrote is from my heart. I'll whisper the lines into Master's ears. He'll know why:

Just to remind you that I'm near,
Sometimes you'll find my hair,
A strand or two,
Not clumps I shed
On rugs and floors and all my beds.

Now that I reside somewhere else,
One plus for sure you can't ignore:
You don't have to
Stuff your pockets
With poop bags for me anymore.

Next time you go for a long walk
For old times' sake, I hope you'll talk;
Pretend I'm there;
Trust me, I'll hear
If my leash is in your pocket.

Ahead

"Arf! Arf! Arf!"

It sounded like Alfie calling out to me in the distance.

I left the house, penetrating the locked front door, relieved once more that no good-byes were said. There was no need. I was determined to return again and again, drawn back home by memories—theirs and mine.

I ascended and reentered the cool, fluffy haze where Alfie's scent seemed to fade in and out. Was he on the move? I strained to get a whiff of my pooch pal. I guess he had decided not to wait for me any longer. When I left him, I hadn't intended to stay away as long as I did.

I turned my nose upward to check the area. Alfie's trail seemed to move back toward the Scioto River, in the direction where the sun first appeared every morning.

In the mist before me and off to my left, I saw the faint outline of a large dog nuzzling another at shoulder height. Was it Alfie and Dexter? I tilted my head. No. The shapes of their heads and bodies were wrong and their smells were unfamiliar.

My air bed shifted beneath me, veering further east. As I crossed the river, I looked down, past the haze. The men with the poles and the birds were gone. So was the sun. A few raccoons walked along the water's edge.

I paused, wondering if my nose had failed me. Was I tracking Alfie's new movements or retracing the path we took from the field in order to return to my home? Both trails seemed fresh.

I remembered what Mistress always said whenever she faced a challenge was, "Keep going. Never give up." I used to think she did that only because she was as stubborn as the burro who lived at Camp Woof. Maybe she was right. I had to continue searching. I had to find Alfie.

My cloud bed pushed forward. As I approached packs of resting dogs on my left, I slowed to exchange nods and to sniff and scan the crowd. Alfie's scent was weak but noticeable in the heavy air. He had passed that way and had moved on. I had to do the same.

Before long, the scenery and the smells changed. Smoke from cars and homes and restaurants blew upward. Exhaust. Wood. Beef. Then, I caught a whiff of something else. On the other side of a dense fog patch, there he was, facing me, sitting upright.

My cloud pillow stopped alongside his.

Alfie, I'm sorry.

Apology accepted, but it is quite unnecessary. You had things to do. So, did I.

I only left you so I could go home. I needed to check on my human mom and dad. Their bodies seemed to be fine but they smelled, sounded, and looked really sad. I've got to find them another dog.

Sounds like the right thing to do, mate.

I've written an ad listing all the things the dog should be. Do you want to hear it?

That's unnecessary. I'm fairly certain you plan to find a dog very much like you.

In some ways. Actually, I think Master would prefer to

have a Lab like you. He had one once.

The man obviously has impeccable taste. How do you intend to locate your replacement?

The same way I'm going to help you find Dex. With my superior schnoz.

Right. Remember, you're—we're—up here, among dog spirits. The dogs who live and breathe and, of course, do other things we used to do, are down there.

I know that. Finding another dog might not be simple, but I'll do it. I really want Master and Mistress to be happy again. The dog will have to be as charming as me but needs to look totally different. I don't want my fans to be confused.

It seems you've got your plans fairly sorted. Now, look down, Samson.

I recognized the woods and ballfields where Alfie and I had enjoyed many walks and adventures. The area bustled with people chatting while dogs of all sorts sniffed and played off-leash, grateful to have found human parents and homes where they could give and get plenty of love.

As the sun disappeared, I lowered my eyes and snout, eager to resume my Doggy Detective role. I had two big cases to solve.

Easing Skyward

Before I left our home, I also left this note for Mistress Carmen to pass along to my beloved doggy doctors, Kellogg and Moeller:

Thank you for caring for me after I became an Ambrosio.

You were so kind and generous. How could I not forgive you after every needle, poke, prod, teeth scrubbing, and toe nail pruning I endured? I knew tasty treats and extra special attention would be coming my way after any brief suffering.

Throughout the years, I appreciated your soothing touch and mellow tone more and more as my hips stiffened and my kid-knees (sorry, I never grasped that word) decided to fail.

I am grateful, too, for the compassionate and patient ways

165

you counseled my human mom and dad through the final, horrible days I felt, and they watched, my health decline.

Only then did you speak the truth my troubled eyes revealed: when food mattered to me no more, the end of my Earth life was near.

How many times have you had to manage pet parent expectations and speak instead of scheduling death? It must make you sad each time you have to prepare human moms and dads to say goodbye to a four-legged family member before they return home, vacant leash in hand, to face empty bowls and beds.

When the moment for my transition came, you made my spirit's journey from land to sky serene and swift. Then, you allowed Master and Mistress ample time and space to release showers of tears.

I hope memories of my wagging tail and Beagle-mutt songs bring you and them smiles when you need joy most.

Aloft

Now that my shift skyward is complete, I say this to Mistress, Master, Brian, and my other dedicated fans:

> In the years to come,
> as the wound of my physical absence
> aches and scars your hearts—
>
> Please know
> my spirit rides the wind,
> I no longer feel pain,
> and I'm right tail wagging again.
>
> Woof!

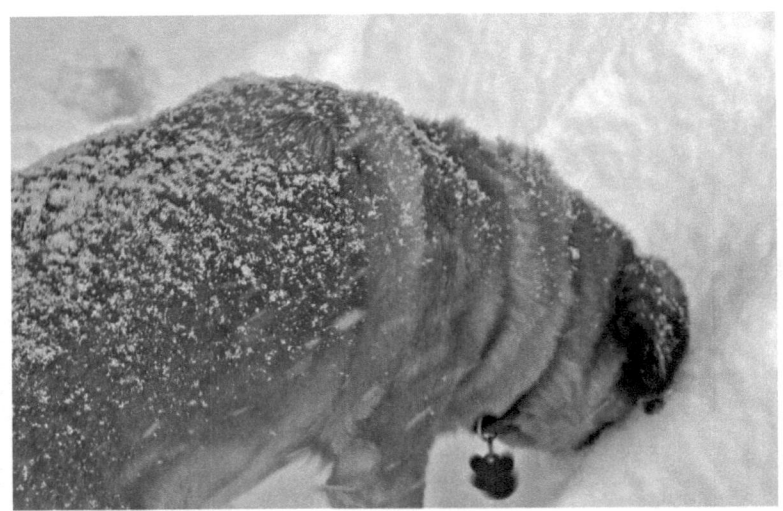

Perfect Imperfection

Final Thoughts from Mistress Carmen

Sam deserved to be pampered for he never chewed shoes, unearthed plants, devoured defrosting meat, or barked himself hoarse. He also waited and waited and waited extra hours on those rare days when we came home late and his evening walk was delayed.

Most impressive was how my favorite mutt could wrap me around his paws. *Please,* his eyes would plead. *The ears. Start my massage there.* Because I was incapable of declining that wish, I would submit. My fingers would stroke the crown of his head before caressing the length of each silky, dark chocolate

169

ear. Satisfied, he would sigh and shrug, then turn to face me, demanding I plunge my hands further back, into the dense hair of his neck and shoulders. Far too soon—at least to Sam—my fingers would tire and his massage would end, prompting protests and pleas for me to reconsider. I rarely refused.

I suspected he knew he could coerce me to do, and to forgive, almost anything he did. When he pressed his nose against the back door as his weekly *GREENIES* dangled from his lips like a stogie, pleading for me to allow him to savor his treat in the grass, I usually gave in. If he whimpered and puked at 2:30 a.m., I never failed to hear him or hesitate to abandon my bed to attend to his needs. Most times that meant feeding him slices of bread or letting him outside to get a dose of nature's canine antacid, grass. Hours later, if his tummy still churned, I would boil chicken or turmeric-flavored rice to feed him. More than once, he persuaded me to pretend I still lived in the frozen tundra called Buffalo and don sweaters, leggings, wool socks, ski headband, hat, and a bulky parka just so he could romp in a snow bank as sleet pelted us both. I would stand shivering, to marvel as he scooped fresh snow into his open mouth while he ran, like a plow powered by four legs. I might grumble, but I indulged him for as long as my throbbing ears and frozen nose could bear because the joy on his face was worth the pain.

Postscript

Sam's absence from our household left a hollowness much deeper than I had anticipated the void would be. Before I could begin to write this book, I needed years to grieve. Imagining how Sam might relate his experiences of the time we spent together elicited laughter and tears.

I regret that I didn't start photographing him until roughly seven years after we found each other, a time when his swagger and spunk had begun to decline. Because I prefer to be on the other side of the camera lens, few images exist of me with him. None of those appear in this book. Nevertheless, I hope the pictures I've included convey some of the qualities that made our four-legged family member special.

Though Larry and I long to hear Sam's incomparable Beagle-Labrador-Whatever mutt song and revel in his other eccentricities again, as long as we cherish the lasting impact of his presence, we never have to say good-bye.

Perhaps, one day we will welcome another dog into our hearts and household, but only when Sam finds one for us.

Acknowledgements

For suggesting I transform Samson's occasional dog blog into a full-length book, I thank Ohio writer Francoise Bartram.

I am grateful to my lunch mates, author colleagues, and early manuscript readers Rosalie Ungar, Margie Hiermer, and Elizabeth Sammons for their friendship and encouragement as my ideas evolved, pivoted, stalled, and inched forward.

Hugs go to Elizabeth Kellogg and Paula Moeller, Doctors of Veterinary Medicine, who cared for Samson, and reviewed the euthanasia sequence of this book for technical accuracy.

For their invaluable perspective and candid feedback as passionate dog moms and Beta manuscript readers, I thank pals Janine Moon and Marti Boyce.

I am deeply indebted to my sister-in-law Pat Rodeawald for her time, expertise, patience, and uplifting counsel. She willingly took on the multiple roles of Beta Reader, Supreme Typo Finder, and Grammar Guru once again.

For solving the most confounding aspect of relating my tale in an eleventh hour save, I am extremely grateful to Jim Ambrosio, my brother-in-law and accomplished writer, journalist, and editor.

Finally, my enduring affection and appreciation goes to Larry (a.k.a. Sir Lawrence James), my infinitely patient and understanding husband, who introduced Samson into our lives and was instrumental in helping me craft this story. He also tolerated my frequent, middle-of-the-night, fumbling for paper, and noisy scribbling without complaining. That's love.

About the Author

Carmen Ambrosio is a writer and an art photographer who was born in St. Thomas, U. S. Virgin Islands.

SAMSON: Memories of a Found Hound is her second book. Her memoir, *Life Continues: Facing the Challenges of MS, Menopause, and Midlife with Hope, Courage, and Humor,* was published in 2010.

The certainty of the uncertainty inherent in having multiple sclerosis (MS) increases the urgency for her to write and create art while she can.

Carmen and her husband Larry live in Central Ohio.